Please return/renew this item by the
last date shown to avoid a charge.
Books may also be renewed by phone
and Internet. May not be renewed if
required by another reader.

www.libraries.barnet.gov.uk

For my mum, Bibi,

who chose England for my Girls' Rights

First published in the UK by Scholastic Children's Books, 2022
Euston House, 24 Eversholt Street, London, NW1 1DB
A division of Scholastic Limited

SCHOLASTIC and associated logos are trademarks and/or
registered trademarks of Scholastic Inc.

Text copyright © Sufiya Ahmed, 2022
Cover illustration by Euan Cook, 2022

ISBN 978 0 70231 371 4

Printed and bound by CPI Group (UK) Ltd, Croydon, CR0 4YY
Papers used by Scholastic Children's Books are made from wood
grown in sustainable forests.

2 4 6 8 10 9 7 5 3 1

While this book is based on real characters and actual historical events,
some situations and people are fictional, created by the author.

www.scholastic.co.uk

Chapter 1

Voyage to a Lost Kingdom

1886

The gust of wind swoops down and blows my hair up all around my face.

My vision is hindered by my unruly, dark curls and fear fills me as I realize I must let go of the ship's railing. Thick, long black hair and stormy sea voyages do not go hand in hand. Not when the SS *Verona* is still in European waters, with their temperamental windy weather. I release my tight hold of the metal bar just as another gust of wind forcefully pushes me forward. Shrieking, I stagger, convinced that I shall be thrown overboard and killed at the age of only nine.

"Mama!" I yell.

A firm grip grasps my hand. The fingers are longer than mine and soft, but it is not Mama's hand. It is my eldest sister who takes hold of me.

1

"Steady there, Soph," Bamba says with a hint of amusement. "It's just a bit of wind and water."

I cling to Bamba and call out to my younger brother. He is only six years old and probably as frightened as me. "Eddie!"

"He's fine," Bamba assures me. "Catherine's got his hand. Look!"

I turn my head to see Eddie standing close to my second-eldest sister.

"Honestly, why did you come out on to the deck if you're scared of the sea?" Bamba grumbles. "You should have stayed with Mama."

I say nothing. There is no way Eddie and I would willingly remain locked up in Mama's cabin with her. No, we are far better off following Bamba, Catherine and my two older brothers, Victor and Freddie, around the ship.

We are all aboard the SS *Verona*, a steamship that set sail for India from England. Our journey will last just under four weeks and we will make a few stops along the way. We have already stopped at Gibraltar. There was nothing exciting there to write about in my journal. It was just a blob of land in the middle of the sea. I am looking forward to the stopover in Egypt. Freddie says that is where the pyramids are located, and we will be allowed to visit the ancient site for a few hours before we are on our way again. I cannot wait. I am going to climb on the Sphinx with Eddie and ride a camel in the desert. It is going to be a wonderful adventure.

Bamba, Catherine and Freddie are also enjoying this trip. The only one who is behaving like Mama is Victor, my papa's heir. He has been sullen throughout the voyage. He says he hates this ship and our trip. Just like Mama.

"Dinner time, children." Our Indian nanny, the ayah Maju, steps out on to the deck and visibly shivers. She is dressed in a white sari and cardigan, quite inappropriate clothes for the weather. She wears it as a uniform. There are many other ayahs in white saris travelling on the ship with whole families. Strangely enough, some children are even making the journey with only their ayahs for company. I wonder what it feels like not to have a papa or mama to look after you. Papa employed Maju for this trip. I think it is because he does not think Mama can cope with all six of us children together. He would never admit it though. Instead, he insists that Maju is with us so that she may teach us Punjabi, one of the Indian languages. Although he cannot speak it very well himself, Papa seems mortified that none of his children know his country's language.

Mama is not keen on us learning Punjabi at all and,

unknown to Papa, has forbidden the ayah to teach us. Maju's day consists of following us around the ship.

"You coming?" Maju calls impatiently.

Bamba strides forward, dragging me with her. "Maju, will you tell me more of your stories about India after dinner?"

Maju smiles and nods. She and Bamba have become friends. Maju loves to talk and Bamba is like a dry sponge, soaking up anything and everything about India. Sometimes I think Bamba is more excited about visiting India than Papa is.

In the dining room, the red-coated Indian stewards usher us to the front of the queue. All the Indian crew, who are known as lascars, have been awestruck by us since we set foot on this ship. Their smiles are wide when they see us children and they almost bow to the floor whenever they glimpse Papa.

The head steward leads us towards the captain's table. As members of royalty, we are granted the best seats. Papa is already seated in the second-best chair, right next to the first position of the captain. They are both surrounded by the other rich passengers, who seem fascinated by Papa. They probably think he is a 'colourful, charismatic maharaja'. These are not my words. Bamba says that's how people describe him. She also says he used to be one of

Queen Victoria's favourite people, and that he tried to please her when he was a young boy by converting from his birth religion of Sikhism to Christianity.

Maharaja means 'great king' in the Indian language.

My papa is the Maharaja Duleep Singh of Punjab.

Of course, he does not rule his kingdom.

Queen Victoria's British Empire rules it on his behalf.

The steward holds a chair out for Bamba on the table adjacent to the captain's. We may be princes and princesses, but we are still children and therefore not allowed to sit at the first table.

I glance around for Mama, but she is nowhere to be seen. She has probably asked for her dinner to be delivered to her cabin. Sighing, I take a seat beside Bamba, whilst little Eddie sits to my right, next to Catherine.

"Were you all right on the deck?" he asks me in a worried tone as he lays the crisp, white napkin on his lap.

I smooth the corners of the napkin over his legs. Eddie is always in my shadow and I like to look after him, just as Bamba seems to look after me. It is something that I do now that Mama seems so lost in her own world most of the time. She has been like this ever since she learned about Papa's special lady friend. Her name is Ada and everyone knows that he loves her too, even though he is married to Mama.

Back in England, I once heard Victor tell Bamba that Mama feels betrayed by Papa. I'm not quite sure what to make of it all except that I wish Mama could be happy again, and laugh and sing with me and Eddie like long ago.

The waiters place a bowl of soup in front of each of us. I take my own napkin and place it on my lap. The buzz of conversation at the other tables has dimmed, and now there is only one voice that booms out. It is Papa, ready to give his speech to anyone who will listen.

"I was cheated out of my kingdom, did you know? My father, the Maharaja Ranjit Singh, the Lion of Punjab, died a natural death and then the vultures circled. My mother, the Maharani Jindan, a brave and courageous woman, was dragged off screaming as I, a small boy, was tricked into signing my kingdom away. The great Sikh kingdom of Punjab was gobbled up by the invaders."

There is a small gasp in the dining room.

Bamba tries to hide a smile and whispers. "They don't like being described as invaders, do they?"

She is talking to Victor, who is sitting on her other side. Victor looks like he wants the floor to open and swallow him whole. I have never seen him appear so embarrassed.

If there was a hush in the dining room before, now there is a pin-drop silence. Even the clink of the cutlery on china has stopped. I look over my shoulder at Papa. He looks incredibly pleased to be the centre of attention. Expanding his chest, he continues his rant.

"I was cheated! Cheated, I tell you. But now I have seen the light. I know the truth. The rose-coloured tint has been removed from my sight. Now I see. Now I know my duty to my people. They wait for me. They yearn for me to return and take back my kingdom from the invaders."

The second use of the word 'invaders' triggers another gasp. It seems to me that people are quite shocked at Papa's use of language. Satisfied that he has caused a stir, Papa picks up his spoon to eat. It is a cue for everyone else to continue as well, and soon the dining room is filled with the din of talk and silverware against china bowls.

I scoop the soup into my spoon just as Victor slams his own spoon down with a clunk, splattering the white tablecloth with yellow liquid.

"I can't believe the idiotic parent is at it again," Victor mutters through gritted teeth. "This is why Mama refuses to join us down here. He just shows us up and then people point and laugh at us."

"Shh." Bamba jabs his arm with her finger. "Don't talk like that."

"Why shouldn't I?" he retorts in a low voice. "He's

uprooted us from home and is dragging us halfway across the world to a country we don't know."

"England was never our home," Bamba says furiously, sounding more like Papa with every word. "India is our rightful land and one day you will be the king, the maharaja of that land again."

"I don't want to reclaim a kingdom that means nothing to me," Victor snaps, scraping back his chair noisily. "I want to go home to England!"

The screech on the wooden floor causes two old ladies to tut disapprovingly. Victor doesn't notice as he storms out of the dining hall. No doubt he is headed to Mama. She doesn't want to go to India either. She spends all her time fretting about what Queen Victoria and her court will make of Papa's words about the British Empire.

I like Queen Vi. She is my godmother and the Empress of India.

Chapter 2

The Pyramids

1886

Today is the day I will get to see the pyramids.

The SS *Verona* will soon be docking at Port Said in Egypt. This is where we will be allowed to disembark to explore the local area. I am so excited when I awake in the morning. Eddie and I have been counting down the days for our visit to Giza, where the pyramids are located. It is near the city of Cairo, where Papa and Mama met and married a long time ago.

I am determined that nothing can spoil my day. Not even a repeat of the almighty row that Papa and Mama had last night in her cabin.

"What are they arguing about?" Eddie had muttered, hiding his face in my shoulder.

"Something about Mama supporting him," I whisper. "Papa thinks she doesn't stand by him as she should."

"That's because she doesn't want to go to India," Eddie says. "She and Victor just want to go home."

I bite my lip in annoyance. Mama and Victor really have done all they can to put a dampener on this trip. Why can't they just enjoy it like the rest of us? Why can't they be like Bamba, who is lapping everything up and glowing more and more with each passing day?

Well, I am determined to enjoy this trip, just like Bamba.

Papa stops over at our table during breakfast. I peer closely up at him and notice the anger in his eyes. Papa likes to give the impression that he is always in control but I can tell that he is on edge.

"Wear your best clothes today, children," he says in a tightly controlled voice.

"Best clothes for the pyramids?" Eddie asks excitedly. As the youngest, he hasn't noticed Papa's dark mood. The rest of us sit stiffly in our chairs.

"No, not for the pyramids," Papa declares, dashing mine and Eddie's dream of an Egyptian adventure.

Eddie stares at Papa's back as he walks away. "But—"

"Shh." Bamba places a finger on her lips. "Why did you think we were going to visit the pyramids? Who told you that?"

Eddie points to Freddie.

"I meant it as a joke," Freddie says, shrugging. "I didn't think Eddie would set his heart on it."

I frown at Freddie. He had made it up and Eddie and I had believed him! We were never going to see the pyramids on this trip.

"But Freddie…" Eddie almost wails.

"No more talk of pyramids!" Bamba snaps. "We have bigger problems."

I peer at her closely. Some of that glow she had acquired over the last week seems to have faded. In fact, she looks positively upset today. Bamba knows something. Papa must have confided in her, or she must have eavesdropped on our parents' conversation.

"What's going on, Bamba?" I ask.

She shakes her head, unable to clear the frown marking her face. "Just stay close to me."

An hour later, the SS *Verona* docks at Port Said. There is no line of excited passengers, ready to step off the ship for a few hours. After breakfast, the captain had made an announcement on the loudspeaker that no passengers would be permitted to disembark. He had, however, requested that Papa and our family join him on the main deck.

All around us, the curious eyes of passengers are fixed on the royal Indian family. We are all in our best clothes. I am holding Eddie's hand and my other hand is firmly gripped in Bamba's. Mama is standing in front of us, with Victor and Freddie on either side of her. I can't tell if she is managing to remain upright herself, or if they are holding her up. She looks positively mortified. This is exactly the kind of attention she hates.

Papa is at the head of us all. He is dressed in his finest maharaja clothes. His robe is blood red, strings of pearls are coiled around his neck and yards of red silk are twirled on his head. A single diamond shines in the centre of his turban. Although it is big, it's a poor relative of the Koh-i-Noor, the most precious and most expensive diamond in the world, which used to belong to my grandfather, the Maharaja Ranjit Singh.

The Koh-i-Noor now belongs to my godmother, Queen Vi. The English soldiers took it from my grandfather's treasury and gifted it to the queen without the permission of anyone in our family.

I do not understand what is going on. Eddie grasps my hand and I squeeze it reassuringly. Father looks like he wants to do battle with the Englishman walking slowly up the gangplank. He looks dull and boring in his dark suit. He comes to a stop a few feet from Papa.

"Maharaja Duleep Singh, sir," he says in a calm voice. "My name is Colonel Hogg. I am a representative of the Crown, based in Aden in Yemen. I have travelled here to meet with you at the instruction of the Viceroy of India."

"What's a Viceroy of India?" Eddie whispers.

"It's the man in charge of India for Queen Vi," I reply.

Papa takes a step forward. "There was no need for you to travel so far from Aden just for me."

Colonel Hogg clears his throat. I think he is nervous. Papa looks quite intimidating in his Indian clothes. He is even wearing a dagger on his belt. He told Bamba once that Sikhs were warriors and that she was one too. A *sherni*. A lioness.

"Maharaja, perhaps you do not understand. I am here to prevent you from continuing your journey to India. It is not the Viceroy's wish that you travel to the Punjab. In fact, he forbids it."

"How dare he!" Papa explodes. His roar is so loud that Mama visibly jumps in her spot.

"I am the rightful ruler of Punjab!" Papa bellows. "Who is the Viceroy to tell me what I can and cannot do? It is preposterous. The Viceroy is merely a puppet of the Crown. He is not a king. He is an officer of the Crown. I, on the other hand, am the Maharaja. Royal blood flows in my veins."

13

To his credit, Colonel Hogg holds his ground. Most men would stagger back a few paces in the face of Papa's fury. Not this officer.

"That may be so," he continues in the same calm voice. "But I have my instructions for your arrest. You and your family may leave this ship with dignity, or we can take you all in handcuffs."

A wail escapes Mama. Papa shoots her a dark glance over his shoulder. I raise frightened eyes. The other passengers' eyes are fixed on us. There are expressions of curiosity and even sympathy. Father had informed everyone that we, the rightful royal family of Punjab, were on our way to India to reclaim our kingdom. Our birthright.

On the way we were supposed to see the pyramids, but that dream is over too. Egypt and India: two exotic places that have been denied to me by the busybody types that serve Queen Vi.

Instead of embarking on an adventure, we are being led away as if we are mere criminals. I only have to glance at Bamba's face to know how absolutely humiliating this is. She looks furious. Bamba has always resented the way the British treat the people of India.

"Why are we seen as second class because our skin is brown?" she would ask.

Papa would answer that we will be first class in our land again.

That dream is now shattered. We are not even allowed to travel to our ancestral land. I do not understand why Queen Vi will not allow Papa to rule it. She claims to have been ruling it on his behalf since he was a little boy. Well, he is grown up now.

"My friends!" Papa's voice booms out to the passengers who are staring down at him. "You must be my witnesses. I am being ordered off this vessel against my will. My plans to travel to my rightful homeland with my wife and children are being thwarted. This is injustice!"

I look sideways at my brothers and sisters. Bamba's eyes are shining with defiance. I think if she had her way, she would stand next to Papa and wave her fist in the air in an act of rebellion. Victor is sullen. He looks as if he wants the ship to sink, and us with it. I suppose he should be happy though, as this surely means we will be sailing home again.

Colonel Hogg steps forward and touches Papa's shoulder. I cannot hear what he says but Papa nods. He then turns to Mama. "Let us leave."

We all walk to the gangplank but before Papa steps on it, he turns and shouts to the ogling passengers, "I leave this ship unwillingly. My case will be the subject of a great state trial – before the House of Lords!"

Some of the passengers cheer and we Duleep Singhs walk the plank like criminals. I feel humiliated and sick under the hot North African sun. It is as if I am a character from one of the storybooks I used to read to Eddie. The tale of evil pirates who make the innocent walk the plank before tipping them into the sea.

We, of course, are not tipped into the sea. We are transported to Aden and set up in a house that belongs to the British residency. Colonel Hogg is adamant that we will not be allowed to travel to India. Even worse, he makes it clear that Papa will not be allowed to return to England unless he swears loyalty to the Crown.

"I will do no such thing," Papa retorts to Mr Hogg.

"Then you will not be permitted to return to England," Colonel Hogg mildly replies.

Papa raises his chin in defiance. It is clear that he thinks the Colonel is beneath him and he is enraged that a mere officer is telling him what he can and cannot do. "You won't let me go to India and you won't let me return to England – even though I don't want to. Pray do tell me, Mr Hogg, where am I supposed to go?"

Colonel Hogg is silent.

"Duleep, we have to go back to England," Mama jumps in. "I can't live here in this awful heat with my children. Do something."

Papa curses under his breath. I think this is what he means when he accuses Mama of not supporting him in public.

Mr Hogg's expression turns to one of sympathy as he looks at Mama. "The Maharani and the children may return," he says. "With or without your sworn loyalty to the Crown."

It takes Papa another twelve days to decide to send us home.

Bamba is inconsolable. "Please don't send us back, Papa," she cries, her arms clinging to his neck. "We will find a way to get to India. We will succeed if we stay together."

Mama tries to wrench Bamba away from Papa. "Let him go!"

Papa raises a hand and Mama steps back. He unwraps Bamba's arms and holds her hands in his own. "Listen to me, darling *sherni*, I will find a way back to India and when I get there, I will send for you. We will be together again in my father's palace. I will sit on his throne and we will throw the British out of our land. I promise you."

"No," Bamba wails. "We will be trapped in England for ever if you send us back now."

"Bamba!" Papa snaps. "Enough!"

I want to run to my sister and wipe her tears, as she has always dried mine. But I am too afraid to move from behind Mama. Eddie presses his fingers into my palm. I look down and give him a watery smile.

Papa turns to Victor and Freddie. "I will send for you boys soon."

Freddie nods vaguely but Victor's sullen expression returns. There is no way that Papa's heir will ever travel to India willingly. He says nothing though, as this is not the place for family disagreements.

"I will see you all soon," Papa says gruffly before walking away from us.

I do not think Queen Vi will allow Papa to travel to India.

The question is, will he ever return to England?

The dread building in my tummy is telling me that he will not.

Chapter 3

Mama

1887

I feel my forehead.

It is rather clammy and should be reason enough for me to miss today's event. I just don't think I can face it.

It is Mama's funeral.

How can I go and stand by her coffin when she is dead because of me? I slump down on the bed and try to find the words to say to Catherine. She is adjusting her black hat by the mirror.

In the end, I choose the simplest words. "I'm not coming."

Her hands still and she gazes at me through the glass. "What?"

"To the funeral," I say. "I can't."

"Oh, Soph," Catherine says. "It's Mama's funeral. You have to come. She would want you there."

"No," I protest. "She wouldn't."

"And why not?"

"She's dead because of me."

Catherine turns around to face me. "Why do you think that?"

"Because I was the one who was sick with the fever and she caught it when she was looking after me."

Catherine slowly walks to the bed and sits down. "Soph, Mama didn't die because of you. The doctor said she was ill from before because she was drinking too much alcohol, and she also had something called diabetes. That night before she died, she wanted to make sure you were going to get better, so she nursed you for a bit. You were so feverish."

"But they found her lying dead on the floor whilst I slept on the bed."

Catherine gathers me up in her arms. "Darling Soph, it wasn't your fault. Mama was not happy with her life."

"It's Papa's fault that she was unhappy, isn't it?"

Catherine doesn't say anything because I am right. Papa sent us home from Aden and then made his way to Paris to live there. We could not return to our home, Elveden Hall, because it had been sold to pay off Papa's debts.

I miss Elveden Hall so much. It was in the Norfolk countryside and resembled a grand Indian palace with a garden full of animals from India. We had parrots and peacocks and there were even real cages for a leopard and a cheetah. It is all gone now. Sold before we set off for India, leaving us homeless when we returned from Aden.

Alone without Papa in England, we were given a house in London on Queen Vi's orders. It was in Holland Park, bang in the middle of all the society people that Papa had once been friends with. A few months after we'd moved in, I heard Mama crying to someone in the drawing room as I hid on the stairs.

"Can't you do something about the Russians and the Irish who are corrupting the Maharaja's mind?"

Mama is talking about the foreign men who are leading Papa astray. I had heard Mama explaining to Victor about the Russian agents who want to weaken the British Empire, and the Irish republicans who don't want Queen Vi to rule Ireland. They have promised Papa that they will help him restore his kingdom by fighting the British troops in India.

"Your papa is committing treason against Queen and Country," Mama had wailed. "These men are using him to cause trouble for Queen Victoria, but he is too pig-headed to see it."

The man who answered had a deep voice. It was Arthur Oliphant, who had been given the job by Queen

Vi of looking after us. "Do not fret, Maharani. The Crown knows you are not part of his rebellion."

"Are you sure? I mean, my husband has completely abandoned me and my children. We are all innocent of treason."

"Her Majesty is aware of it. She has made it clear that you and the children will be looked after. Victor and Sophia are her godchildren. Her Majesty takes her role of godmother very seriously. She made a vow to care for them in front of God. She wants you to be assured of that."

"Oh, thank God."

"It is not advisable for you to remain in London," Mr Oliphant said. "There is too much gossip about the Maharaja. The Crown has decided that you shall be set up in a home in Kent. It is in the countryside, away from London society."

"Thank you. Thank you."

"But, Maharani." Mr Oliphant's voice was grave. "You must stop the drinking. You are not much of a mother when you are senseless."

"I do it to ease the pain." Mama's voice was small and pitiful.

"Think of your children," Mr Oliphant continued in that grave voice. "They need you."

And so, not long after that conversation, we had moved to Kent. It was here that Mama had died on the floor, whilst I slept.

"Soph," Catherine says. "You have to come to the funeral. It would be odd if you didn't."

The door suddenly bursts open and Bamba storms in. Her eyes are red from tears, but she is wearing an angry expression.

"Why are you two taking so long?" she demands. "The boys are ready and waiting downstairs."

"Soph was just saying that she wasn't feeling too well and…" Catherine's voice trails off as Bamba's face darkens.

Bamba comes to stand directly in front of me, hands on hips. "Now you listen to me, Sophia Duleep Singh. You will get up and attend Mama's funeral. You will not hide away from the world. You will face it with the rest of us. Be assured that as long as Catherine and I are beside you, no one will dare say a word to you. Do you understand?"

I nod meekly.

"Right. Put your hat on and let's go." Bamba marches out of the room.

I grab my hat and follow. Catherine takes my hand and keeps hold of it all day.

Nobody from Papa's old world attends Mama's funeral.

Apart from us, the only mourners are a few villagers and Mr Oliphant, our guardian. No one would ever think this was the funeral of a maharani.

Chapter 4

A Christmas Walk

1889–90

Our family has been separated and it pains my heart every day.

I now live with the Oliphant family in Brighton and attend a day school. My darling Eddie is at a boarding school, Catherine and Bamba are students at Somerville College in Oxford, Victor has just finished training to be an army officer at Sandhurst, and Freddie is at Cambridge.

I miss them all every single day. I have gone from living as one of six children to being an only child. Papa abandoned us and Mama died, but I always thought we brothers and sisters would remain under one roof.

My siblings all travel to the Oliphants' house for Christmas. I've been counting down the days, and when they finally arrive, I embrace each of them in turn. It's so good to see them. I hug Eddie last and marvel at how much he's grown. He tells me that I have too and we hug again. I wonder if I will ever be able to let him go.

Bamba soon parts us. "Come on, you two," she says. "Let's wash hands and eat. I'm so hungry."

We are all so happy to be back together again and spend the days playing games and singing songs. I can play the piano well now, thanks to the music lessons Mr Oliphant insisted I take. I shyly show off my musical skills and my brothers and sisters clap and cheer till I flush a deep, dark red.

Mr Oliphant is especially proud of me and he tells me that Queen Vi will be delighted to learn that I play so well. As my godmother, she sent me a doll for Christmas. I think I'm too old to play with it, but I promise Mr Oliphant that I will pen a thank-you letter. I also thank him and his wife for their presents, as do my siblings. Eddie is especially happy with his new train set.

None of us receive anything from Papa. It is not a shock. He hasn't sent us any gifts, whether for our birthdays or Christmas, for a while now.

It is only when we trudge through the snow to walk off our Christmas lunch that Victor brings up Papa's name. He informs us that Papa has finally given up on the idea of regaining his own kingdom. He has repented and asked the queen to forgive him.

Bamba is furious. "But I thought he was working to return to India as the rightful maharaja."

"All his plans failed," Victor explains with a grim face. "Papa travelled to Moscow and stayed there for months waiting to speak to the Tsar. The Russian agents had convinced him that the Tsar would give him an army to help him overthrow the British and reclaim his Sikh kingdom. But his invitation to the palace in St Petersburg never came."

"Why?" Catherine asked, looking aghast.

Victor sighs heavily. "The Russians had their own plans to weaken the British hold on India. The British Empire is mighty and most of its wealth comes from India. The Russians initially wanted to invade India using Papa as an excuse, but in the end the Tsar decided that he didn't want to start a war with Britain over the Sikh kingdom."

"Traitors!" Bamba's eyes are full of rage.

Freddie shakes his head. "Papa's problem was that he expected others to give him his kingdom. Nobody gives you power. You have to take it."

"Not as easy as that though, is it?" Bamba snaps. "You need allies."

"Well, he didn't have any real friends in the end," Freddie retorts.

Bamba ignores him and turns to Victor. "So Papa just gave up because some Russians let him down?"

Victor sighs again. "You know the stroke he had when he returned to Paris left him weak. He still can't use one of his arms. I think he felt vulnerable. I was shocked at the state he was in when I saw him in Paris after he sent for me. It turned out that he wanted me to make a case to Queen Victoria on his behalf."

"And did you do it?" Catherine asks.

"Of course I did," Victor replies. "I wrote down the words that he dictated. He wanted me to take the lead as his heir and the queen's godson."

"What did Papa say?" Catherine is curious.

Victor pulls a piece of paper out of his pocket. "I saved a copy so that I could share it with you. It's important that we all know that Papa regrets the madness he pursued."

We stand still in the snow as Victor unfolds the paper and begins to read.

"May it please Your Majesty, my son Victor is writing this letter from my dictation – I have been struck down by the hand of God and am in consequence quite unable to write it myself. I have been disappointed by everyone in

28

whom I have been led to believe and now my one desire is to die at peace with all men. I therefore pray Your Majesty to pardon me for all that I have done against You and Your government. I throw myself entirely on Your clemency. It seems to me that it is the will of God that I should suffer injustice at the hands of Your people. I can find no one to curse Great Britain and in spite of all her faults and her injustices, God blesses her, makes her great and, when I look at her, I feel that in fighting against Your country I have been fighting against God – I would return to England, were I assured of your free pardon. I am Your Majesty's obedient servant."

Victor folds the paper and slips it back into his pocket. The rest of us are quiet. All that effort wasted for a cause he gave up on in the end.

"So is he coming home, then?" Catherine asks.

"I think Queen Vi will grant him permission this year."

"Will she see him though?" Freddie wants to know.

"I can't tell you that," Victor says with a shrug. "I think she has been very hurt by his behaviour. She loved him like a son and called herself his mother. I believe his rants against her cut deep, especially as some of her advisors have been telling her for years not to grow so close to him."

Bamba finally explodes. "She only called herself his

mother because she had him snatched from his real mother, Maharani Jindan! It was just guilt!"

Papa may have accepted defeat, but Bamba most certainly will not.

In August, Papa comes to England, just as Victor said he would. He is accompanied by his new wife, Ada, and their daughters Pauline and Irene.

When I first heard that Papa had remarried, I felt a mixture of emotions. Ada has been in Papa's life for a long time. In fact, when he sent Mama and us children back to England from Aden, he went to live with Ada in Paris. I think when I was younger, I hated Ada for taking Papa away from Mama. But Mama is gone now and he can't hurt her any more. I'm not sure how I feel now about meeting my stepmother.

Victor rents a house for the second Duleep family (as Mr Oliphant calls them) in Folkestone and Eddie and I travel there to meet them, accompanied by Mr Oliphant. Despite feeling nervous about seeing Papa again after so long, I try to enjoy the train ride with Eddie. We play card games, and Eddie has me in fits of laughter as he regales me with funny tales of what he and his friends get up to at boarding school. Mr Oliphant pretends not to be interested as he reads his book, but I see his lips twitching at the really hilarious parts.

When we arrive at Folkestone station, Eddie and I throw our arms around Victor, who is waiting for us. He hugs us back and then looks worriedly at Mr Oliphant.

"The house is smaller than we expected it to be and there isn't room for everyone. Eddie and Soph will have to stay with you at the hotel."

Mr Oliphant nods. "Very well."

Eddie doesn't visibly react to this information and I keep my own expression blank, despite the sinking feeling in my stomach. We have come all this way and there is no room for us in Papa's home. I bite my lip and wish that, instead of being here, I was in Germany with Catherine and Bamba. They are travelling with their old governess, Lina, and will miss this opportunity to see Papa. I'm not sure how Catherine felt, but I'm sure Bamba was desperate to see Papa. Unfortunately for her, Mr Oliphant instructed my sisters not to cut their holiday short. As I hid on the stairs, I heard him confiding to Mrs Oliphant that he was worried Papa might incite Bamba to act against the Empire. "I'm not as convinced as Her Majesty that Duleep has truly repented," he said.

Papa's rented accommodation turns out to be a very

pretty and yes, very small cottage overlooking the sea. As we approach the shiny, red front door, it hits me that I am moments away from seeing Papa. Mr Oliphant notices my slowed pace and gives me a small, encouraging smile.

We find Papa in the drawing room. I stare at him. He looks older and larger, and he seems to have lost most of his hair. Seeing us, Papa gets to his feet and opens his arms out wide. Eddie grabs my hand and I squeeze it. Neither of us move. I hear a hiss behind me and Victor gives us both a little push from behind. Eddie and I stumble forward and are swept up into Papa's arms.

"My children!" be booms. "Ada, meet Edward and Sophia."

Our stepmother steps out of the shadows. I notice that her smile does not reach her eyes. Standing on either side of her are my two half-sisters, Pauline and Irene. They gaze up at me with wide eyes.

"How do you do?" Ada says.

Eddie and I respond politely. The two little girls say nothing. We take our seats by the window and Papa begins to question Eddie about his school. He is not so interested in me. I don't mind. I take the opportunity to sit back and observe Ada. I know that she is from a place called Holborn in London. I have never been to that part of the city. I've also heard that she used to be a hotel chambermaid in Mayfair. Well, now she holds the title of maharani, as Mama is dead. I suppose Ada can be described as attractive, but I do not believe that her beauty can match Mama's.

Mama was the daughter of a German white man and an Ethiopian woman. The combination of European and African genes made her a stunning beauty. She had honey-coloured skin, big brown eyes and flowing black hair that reached her waist. In comparison, Ada looks quite ordinary, but that is only my opinion.

My half-sisters are nice enough. They are little girls, and I do not have much to say to them. I wish again that I was with Bamba and Catherine.

Chapter 5

Losing Eddie

1893

Eddie is dying.

He is suffering from pneumonia and has picked up a stomach bug too. Both things combined are killing my little brother. The doctor says there is nothing we can do but keep him as comfortable as possible and wait for the end.

Mr Oliphant has been sending telegrams to Papa every day.

When Papa finally arrives, he sits beside Eddie's bed and summons the rest of us to him. We stand silently as Papa addresses us.

"I am sorry that I have not been here to see you all grow up. I know you all think I abandoned you and your mama. That was not the case. I loved your mama, but

I had a bigger cause to pursue which took me away from being a good husband and father." He stops and his eyes take on a distant look. I wonder if he is thinking about the cause that meant so much to him.

"I had to reclaim the Sikh kingdom," Papa continues. "I had to win it back. I am the son of the great Maharaja Ranjit Singh and Maharani Jindan. It was my birthright. It was what I had to pass to you." His gaze falls on his eldest son, but Victor refuses to meet his eyes. Papa's heir has never made a secret of the fact that he wants nothing to do with Punjab, whether to rule it or otherwise.

"I tried to reclaim what was mine." Papa's voice has a bitter tone to it now. Perhaps it is the lack of support from Victor that has darkened his mood. "I was used and lied to by devious powers. It took me a while to realize it, but the British Empire is too mighty. Nothing and nobody can defeat it. Certainly not this old, grey maharaja."

"We don't have to accept it," Bamba whispers in a furious tone.

Papa holds up his hand to silence her. "You were always my true heir, my beautiful *sherni*. I knew my own mother only briefly, yet from what I remember of her, she was just like you. Full of fire, full of defiance. You have her spirit, my precious daughter."

I sneak a look at Bamba. She looks like she wants to cry tears of joy for this recognition. All her life, Bamba has been called a troublemaker and a haughty, ill-mannered princess. And here is Papa, referring to her as the spirit of his brave mother who had the courage to defy and fight the English soldiers as they took over her ancestral land.

I glance at Victor. His face is frozen. Papa had just called Bamba his heir. Well, Victor cannot have it both ways. He can't reject Papa's dreams and still expect to be lauded as his true heir.

"I am not here to talk about my failures," Papa says, suddenly weary. "I am here to say sorry for all that you have suffered because of me."

It is an apology from a father to his children. I want him to say more. I want him to also apologize for the way he treated Mama. To apologize for the fact that Mama drank herself to death because he broke his marriage vows to her. To apologize for leaving Mama and us for a hotel chambermaid.

Bamba clears her throat. "Papa, I have a question."

My head shoots up. Perhaps Bamba will demand an apology on behalf of Mama.

Papa smiles at her. "Yes, my *sherni*?"

"Have you converted back to Sikhism?"

I stare, appalled, at Bamba. What are these words coming out of her mouth? Sikhism is the religion that Papa was born into. When he first arrived in England, he converted to Christianity at the request of Queen Victoria. We have all been raised as Christians. Mama was one too. That is why she is buried in the graveyard of an English church.

"I've heard rumours that you have renounced Christianity to embrace your father's religion once again," Bamba finishes.

Papa holds his head high. "It is true. I am a Sikh."

Victor draws a sharp breath but before he can say anything, Catherine jumps in. "We are here for Eddie. No more conversation."

She is right. We turn our attention to Eddie and try to soothe him as he lies there. We tell him tales of all the fun we've had together. Papa slowly rises to his feet and leaves the room. Perhaps he feels left out because he does not feature in any of our stories. It is just us children again. The six of us, as it has always been.

A few days later, Papa picks up Eddie's infection. Feeling unwell, he decides that he will return to Paris to get better.

"Eddie hasn't even passed away yet," I say bitterly as we watch Papa climb into his carriage.

"I do not wish to burden you all with having to look after me," Papa says, having heard my objection. "Look after each other."

Bamba is the only one who remains outside to watch Papa's carriage hurtle away.

Eddie only lives for a few more days.

"I love you, Soph," he tells me the night before he dies. "You're my favourite."

"And you're mine," I whisper, trying to hold back my tears.

His poor lungs finally collapse the next morning and my darling little brother is no more.

This is the second family funeral we shall have to hold without Papa. We decide that Mama's baby must rest beside her.

And so he does, six years after Mama died.

Chapter 6

Empress of India

1893

Despite the high ceiling of the room in Buckingham Palace, it is warm from the roaring fire.

The old lady looks tiny in the chair beside the fireplace. The orange-red flames give her pale, wrinkled skin a slight glow. She is dressed in full black. A widow still mourning her dead husband, even though it's thirty-two years since his death.

My own clothes are dark too. I wear them to mourn Papa.

Papa died on the night of 21 October 1893. Freddie travelled to Paris to bring Papa's body back to England. Although Papa had confessed to us that he had converted back to Sikhism, Victor decided that he should have a Christian funeral. "We'll bury him in Thetford, the same as Mama and Eddie."

We all agreed and so the Maharaja Duleep Singh was buried in the graveyard a short distance from Elveden House, the palace he had built that was fit for a maharaja and which he'd had to sell to pay off his debts.

Both my parents are gone now, but it is my younger brother that I miss the most. It seems as if my shadow has left me.

Today, I have been invited to have tea with my godmother, Queen Victoria, whom I have always referred to as Queen Vi. A maid brings in a silver tray.

"Would you like to pour, little Sophia?" Queen Vi asks.

I am seventeen years old, and she still refers to me as 'little Sophia'.

Shuffling forward in my chair, I lean over the tray and prepare the tea. I know just how Queen Vi likes it. I have poured it for her many times before.

"We were distressed to learn about poor Duleep," she says, sadness tinging her voice. She is one of the few people in the world to call him by his name. The other is her eldest son, Edward, Prince of Wales. He was Papa's best friend and often stayed with us at Elveden House. We know him as Uncle Bertie.

Of course, that was before Papa decided that he hated the queen and her heir for robbing him of his kingdom.

"He was very foolish to think the Russians would help him," Queen Vi says, shaking her head. "Our poor, gullible Duleep was taken in by their empty promise to restore his lost kingdom. Why did he doubt that the British Empire rightfully rules?"

I say nothing as I hand her the cup of tea.

"We forgave your papa," she continues, taking a small sip. She always refers to herself as 'we' to highlight that she speaks for the whole of Britain and the one-fifth of the world that she rules. "We are glad he asked for our forgiveness. Bertie forgave him too. Duleep came to his senses in the end. One man cannot rise up against Britannia. It is extremely easy to have one's ears filled with nonsense. He was led up the garden path by those Russians."

My lips tighten at the mention of the Russians. Such mischief-makers. I do hate them for polluting Papa's mind with impossible dreams. Queen Vi is right. The British Empire is mighty and no one can stand up against it.

"I did not give an audience to the new wife," she reveals. "Scandalous woman for stealing your papa away from his lovely maharani. Your mama was such a shy and pious woman. She did not deserve to be treated like that. Abandoned by her husband for another woman and left with six little children to rear. It is a good thing we were at hand to help her."

"We are very grateful," I say humbly.

"You Duleep Singhs are very precious to me," Queen Vi says, her voice suddenly gentle. "More than you know."

I can only stare at her, unsure what to say.

"It brings me much sorrow to see you children without your mama and papa."

"I still have Victor, Freddie, Bamba and Catherine," I mumble. I do not mention the passing of Eddie and neither does the queen. I wonder if she has forgotten that the sixth and youngest child of her dear friend Duleep has died.

"Indeed, you do have your brothers and sisters," she says. "And we will do all we can to make sure you are cared for. Duleep was incredibly special to me. He was one of my favourites."

We sit in awkward silence until she changes the subject.

"And how are you, little Sophia?"

"I am well," I reply. "I enjoy music and dancing, and Mr Oliphant says I am one of the best horsewomen he has seen and…" My voice drifts off as the queen's attention is diverted to the door.

A servant walks in. He is Indian, tall and with a broad

chest. Indian servants are not new in the palace. Queen Vi has been served by many of them in the times that I have visited her. This man, however, is the first of these servants that Queen Vi has looked up to and smiled at like that.

"Little Sophia, let me introduce you to my Munshi-ji, Abdul Karim."

"Good afternoon, Princess," the man says, bowing his head.

"Good afternoon," I mutter.

"Munshi-ji means 'teacher' in Hindustani," the queen says warmly. "Did you know that, Sophia?"

"Hindustani?" I repeat.

"It's actually Urdu," Munshi-ji says softly, as if expecting me to know.

"I do not know Urdu, Punjabi or any other Indian language," I say.

"Of course you don't," Queen Vi says dismissively. "Why would you?"

I feel a pang of resentment at her implication. I will never need to use Indian languages, especially Punjabi, because I will never be allowed to visit India.

"Have you ever been to India, Munshi-ji?" I ask curiously.

Queen Vi and Munshi-ji laugh.

"Dear Princess," he says. "I am *from* India."

"What's it like?"

"It is the most beautiful land. It has a hot climate, so we never feel the cold. Everywhere you look, there are colourful satins and silks. The air is filled with the aromas of spices and it is the home of the heavenly fruit."

"Heavenly fruit?" I ask, perplexed. What on earth is that?

He nods mysteriously, but reveals nothing.

Queen Vi giggles like a little girl. "Oh, tell her."

"The mango," Munshi-ji declares dramatically, curving his right hand around an invisible fruit. "It is the sweetest, most delectable piece of flesh that you will ever taste. The sweet flavour will burst on your tongue, making your mouth water for more even as you eat it."

I stare in fascination at Munshi-ji. Mango? I have never heard of such a thing. Papa had never mentioned mangoes. Perhaps he had forgotten about them as he had been forced to leave India when he was still a young boy.

"I would like to eat one, please," I blurt out, my mouth watering.

"It is not in our fate," Queen Vi says quietly.

I can't work out if she means me and her, or just her.

"We too have yearned to taste this heavenly fruit, but it is not to be," she adds.

"Why?" I do not understand why she has been denied this. After all, she is the queen.

"I have ordered shipments of the mango many times," Munshi-ji explains. "Alas, the fruit has always rotted completely by the time it reaches these shores. The ants have feasted magnificently on the mango's sweet flesh, leaving only the stone pit for Her Majesty."

"I want to go to India to taste it," I declare.

Queen Vi sighs. "We do too, Sophia. But I am afraid it is not allowed for either of us."

This is news to me. Who can stop the queen from doing what she wants? She's the queen. "Why can't you go?"

"They would kill me," she says simply.

My mouth falls open again. "Why?"

"Because we are the Empress of India and there are people there who do not believe in our right to rule them."

In this very moment I do not care who rules who, for I am overcome with the need to taste a mango. "But you must let me go, Your Majesty, and I can taste it for both of us."

Another heavy sigh and she sits back in her chair. Munshi-ji steps to the side, obedient servant that he is.

"I'm afraid it's out of the question, Sophia," Queen Vi says in a resigned tone. "It would not be safe."

"For me?"

"For the Empire. You live here and we rule in your family's place. If you set foot in India, the people might decide they want you, not us, to rule them. They might rise up against us. It is safer for everyone concerned for the Duleep Singh children to live here under our watch. Safer for the Empire and the people of India. It is the price we must pay for peace."

Chapter 7

Coming Out in Society

1895

The girl in the glass stares back at me, wide-eyed with nerves.

It is my own reflection in the window of a Buckingham Palace drawing room. The white gown fits me like a glove. The waist is cinched, emphasizing my slender frame against the big, puffy sleeves. My white gloves reach my elbows and I clutch a pretty Chinese fan in one hand. Two pearl chokers are fitted around my neck. The pearl at the centre of one of the chokers is the size of a grape and digs into the base of my throat. It is uncomfortable and I try not to move my neck too much.

The headdress that was fastened on by the hairdresser this morning is starting to feel heavy. There is a lot of material coiled around the centre of my head; a veil then flows down all the way to my heels. I have ostrich feathers and white roses resting on top of my head. And why not? After all, today is my debut into London society.

All girls from the aristocracy must 'come out in society'. It is a way of advertising that they are now of an age to be married and that proposals of marriage, from the men of the best families, would be welcome.

Bamba and Catherine are by my side, too, with their own ostrich-feathered veils. They both should have come out years ago when they became of marriageable age, but their debuts were delayed due to Papa's fallout with Queen Vi. Better late than never, I suppose. I can't help the feeling of excitement in my tummy. It is as if there are a hundred butterflies fluttering around. I feel like a real princess. Wait, that doesn't even make sense. I *am* a real princess. I mean I feel like a fairy-tale princess. Like Cinderella going to the ball. I wish Mama were here. She would be so proud of us.

I glance sideways at Bamba and cannot help thinking that her dress reflects her personality. It is luxurious and showy, demanding attention. Catherine's gown is less fussy, much like her, with elegant embroidery at the hem.

I wonder if people will think my dress is a reflection of me. In that case, it should have patterns of horses and dogs all around the skirt for that is all I care about these days.

Noise from the main hall filters through to us.

"What's happened?" Bamba is craning her neck to see. "I can't tell."

Gradually the voices calm down and hushed whispers travel down the line to us. "A girl fainted in front of the queen!"

"Poor thing," Catherine sympathizes. "Who is it?"

"A weak thing, no doubt," Bamba says dismissively. She fixes me and Catherine with a direct look. "Remember that we cannot let the side down. We are the Duleep Singhs, daughters of a maharaja. No tripping and no fainting."

I sneak a glance at Catherine from under my lashes.

"Not even if we wanted to," Catherine mutters.

I am just about to reassure Bamba that we won't embarrass her when I am startled by the announcement of my name.

"Princess Sophia Duleep Singh."

I am being called. I repeat the mantra that I have prepared for today.

Look elegant. Look graceful.

Look elegant. Look graceful.

Look elegant. Look graceful.

I float into the room and a small gasp escapes me. Queen Vi is right at the other end, sitting still as a statue.

The huge room is the size of one of the fields where Papa used to play polo with his friends. The Prince of Wales is up there too, and he recognizes me as I approach. A small smile curves his lips. At any other time, I would have waved at him. He is the familiar honorary uncle who was always at our house. Of course, I do not wave. Instead, I clutch my fan and continue to glide towards the Queen-Empress who is seated on her small throne.

I curtsy low, managing not to stumble, then rise as gracefully as I can. As god-daughter to the queen, I am expected to do one more thing. I step forward and kiss both her cheeks. As I step back, I catch the look of affection in Queen Vi's eyes. She holds my gaze for a moment.

"You look lovely, my dear," she says. "We shall make sure that you are invited to every ball and engagement in London. Duleep would have wanted that for his girls."

And then my moment is over. I bow my head and back out of the room, repeating my mantra.

Look elegant. Look graceful.

At last I am through the tall, wide doors and I want to both shout for joy and crumple to the floor at the same time.

I have arrived in London society.

Chapter 8

No more Duleep Singhs

1898

I am covered in confetti.

Helping a bride into her carriage can do that. I don't mind all the paper that is caught in my hair. At least it is not like the old days when they threw rice grains or sweets at the bride! But I think even then I wouldn't mind because I love the bride so much and I'm so excited about our new family member. She is my new sister-in-law, Lady Anne, who has married my eldest brother, Victor. And the best families in England have turned up for their wedding, making it one of the grandest society occasions of the year.

"We shall see each other as soon as Victor and I return from our honeymoon," Anne says, kissing my cheek.

I nod happily, basking in her affection. We have become such good friends since the engagement was announced.

51

She is only two years older than me and we both love the same things: dogs, horse riding and clothes. Victor has even joked that Anne is more interested in spending time with me than him.

The carriage door shuts, the horses are whipped, and the bride and groom are off to their honeymoon destination. None of us knows where they are going as Victor has planned a surprise.

"Is it Punjab?" Bamba had asked dryly a few days ago.

"Don't be silly," Victor laughed.

The carriage is only a few feet away when Anne's strawberry-blonde head pops out of the window. "Goodbye!"

"Good luck!" Bamba calls.

"Safe journey!" says Freddie.

"Be good!" Catherine shouts.

More goodbyes are yelled out.

I stand in place and continue to wave, not wanting the day to end. It has been such a wonderful wedding. I am so pleased that Victor has finally been able to marry his true love. Anne is the daughter of the Earl of Coventry, who was not willing to permit the marriage when Victor first asked Anne to marry him.

Bamba told me that Uncle Bertie, the Prince of Wales,

intervened to convince the Earl. Uncle Bertie has always looked out for us. He is truly Papa's friend. I think he might also have been acting on the instructions of Queen Vi, as Victor is her godson.

Bamba wasn't very kind about the whole thing as usual. She didn't think that the Earl was refusing the match because of Papa's rebellious ways.

"It's because the Earl doesn't want his white English blood to mix with brown Indian blood. Even though he is only an earl, and Victor is a maharaja and far outranks minor English aristocracy," Bamba had said bitterly.

I wasn't quite sure how to respond to that. It does not matter anyhow. The Earl gave his permission in the end. Queen Vi and Uncle Bertie always take care of us.

I do love music and dancing, but right now I feel I need the tranquillity of the garden at Buckingham Palace rather than the glamour of the packed ballroom. Victor and Anne had returned from their honeymoon early, and my brother was seething with fury. I have never seen him so irate.

It turns out that his secret honeymoon destination was British Ceylon. Alas, the Empire authorities would not allow Victor and his bride to set foot in the capital,

Colombo, even though it is hundreds and hundreds of miles away from Punjab. It was a most humiliating thing to do to a person, and so much worse that it was in front of his English wife.

It is also a horrible reminder of what happened when Papa tried to take us to India all those years ago, and Colonel Hogg ordered us off the steamship in Port Said. We had not even been allowed to see the pyramids.

Bamba didn't know why Victor was so shocked at his treatment.

"Why did he think the son would get treated differently to the father?" she asked me and Catherine. "There is no way that the British Empire will ever allow Maharaja Ranjit Singh's male heir anywhere near India."

Victor made his outrage clear to anyone and everyone who would listen. I think the news must have reached Queen Vi's ears because she has invited Victor and Anne to this state ball at Buckingham Palace. Freddie and I are also invited. So here I am in the palace garden in my lovely new gown, after having danced with so many dashing young men inside.

The trouble is, I feel guilty. I can't quite enjoy the evening for the simple reason that my sisters were not invited. Bamba and Catherine's absence is conspicuous.

Some people have even enquired after them. These people, busybodies all of them, know that Queen Vi did not invite my sisters and they just want to rub it in. I know that some of them do not mind Catherine, but many hate Bamba as much as she hates them. They are not used to being openly mocked or looked down upon by an Indian person, even if she is a princess. Although a deposed one, as some people like to remind her.

I think I shall remain out here under the stars for a while. Actually, I think I will leave. I should not have come. Not when my own sisters were so obviously left out.

A few weeks later, I am sitting in Victor's drawing room, having been let in by a servant, when Anne bursts through the door and stares at me in surprise.

I do not think she expected me to be here.

"Victor invited me for dinner," I blurt out.

"Oh yes," she mutters.

I look closely at her as she walks into the drawing room. Her eyes are red, and she is dabbing her nose with a handkerchief.

"Have you been crying, Anne?" I ask quietly.

She looks at me, ready to deny it, then changes her mind and collapses on the red velvet sofa.

"Anne!" I cry, running to her. "Whatever's the matter?"

She lifts her head from the cushion, and I can see the fresh tears that have made her cheeks wet.

"Oh, Soph," she sobs. "I can't bear it."

"What? What's happened?"

Anne blows her nose into the handkerchief. The tip of her nose is quite red now. I pat her back awkwardly in an attempt to comfort her.

"I was invited to Buckingham Palace today by the queen," she says in a hoarse voice.

I nod.

"She informed me that Victor and I should never have children."

I blink. "What?"

She nods and her voice trembles. "She... she commanded me to never have his children."

"Why?" I ask the question even though I have already guessed the answer.

"I don't know," Anne admits. "But she's the queen and I shall have to obey."

Anne breaks down again and I offer her my shoulder. Poor Anne. She cannot understand why the queen has commanded it, but I can. Victor is the Punjab kingdom's heir. The British Empire does not want any more Duleep

Singhs being born and running around the world threatening its hold on Punjab.

Perhaps the Earl of Coventry had a point when he did not want his daughter to marry a Duleep Singh. After all, don't fathers only want happiness for their daughters?

Life is not all about fairy-tale weddings. Life is all about finding happiness for the rest of it.

Chapter 9

The Sisters' Plan

1902

Catherine picks up a slice of fruit cake and takes a bite. "Mmmm."

We are in my home at Faraday House in the estate of Hampton Court Palace. It was the favourite palace of Henry VIII. It is said that he charmed both Anne Boleyn and Catherine Howard here. Poor women. I bet they didn't think the man wooing them with poems and gallantry would end up chopping their heads off.

Queen Vi gifted Faraday House to me before she died. My godmother lived until the age of eighty-one. I did not get to see her near the end. They say she was very weak. I would have liked to have seen her one last time, but she only permitted very few members of her family to be with her. And of course, her Munshi-ji, Mr Abdul Karim.

We have heard all sorts of rumours about how close Queen Vi was to him. People say she used to refer to herself as his mother and always expressed how much she wanted to visit India. My sisters and I share that desire. People talk of it as a magical land with great big elephants, majestic tigers and beautiful peacocks. It is never cold, dark or cloudy, but always shimmering in the brightest sunlight.

I remember, on the day I met him, Munshi-ji's description of his homeland. He had talked about the colours. Beautiful, bright shades of orange, yellow, blue, red and green. I heard that he was sent back to India after Queen Vi died. She was at Osborne House, on the Isle of Wight, when she breathed her last. It was her favourite place in the world. She died on 22 January 1901. Uncle Bertie was with her. He is now the new King-Emperor, Edward VII.

I am grateful that Queen Vi ordered my accommodation for me when she was alive. Uncle Bertie was always Papa's friend, but I doubt he has the mind to be as considerate as Queen Vi. She also added Bamba's and Catherine's names to the lease on Faraday House. Typically, they hate it here and preferred to move their belongings to Freddie's new country house.

Catherine finishes the last crumb on her plate. I offer her a second slice, but she declines. Instead, she reaches out and picks up the magazine lying on the coffee table. She flicks through and her smile broadens. "Look at you. There are three different pictures of you in this magazine. At a ball in that new gown by the designer you love, at the races in the royal box and at the canine show with your dogs. I heard that you're now one of the most photographed women in England. Quite the star."

I beam back. "Those photographers just follow me around. I spend most of my time with my dogs."

Catherine glances at the corner where two of my prized pets are snoozing. She is not a dog person at all. "How many do you have now?"

"Well, if you count…"

My voice drifts off as Bamba bursts into the room in her typical chaotic style. She collapses on the sofa beside me and sticks her feet up on the coffee table. She is like many of the new women of the twentieth century, thinking she can compete with men in mannerisms and talk.

"I bumped into that awful woman outside," she declares.

I have no idea who Bamba means. There are not many people who can escape her label of 'awful'. I raise my eyebrows in question.

She rolls her eyes in reply. "You know, that one who is the widow of that awful general."

Many women who live on the Hampton Court estate are widows whose husbands died in service to the country.

"I need a name, Bamba," I tease.

"Who knows, but I tell you, little sister, you are living amongst the enemy. All these widows' husbands killed Indians in India."

"Yes, they put down local rebellions," I say. "They were fighting to keep the peace."

Bamba and Catherine exchange a glance and then both roll their eyes.

"So naive," Bamba scoffs at me.

"England is our home," I insist.

"It needn't be," Bamba retorts.

"Anyway," Catherine says, looking to change the subject. "What was so urgent that you insisted we meet in the middle of the week, Bamba?"

Bamba sits up and pulls out a white envelope from her bag. "Look at this!"

"What is it?" I ask.

Bamba suddenly jumps up to dance around my sitting room. The dogs, pulled out of their slumber, begin to bark. The teacup in my hand wobbles and Catherine shakes her head. This is all too chaotic for my calm and serene sister.

"Bamba!" I protest.

She throws the envelope in the air and poses, hands on hips. "It's from old Hamilton."

Bamba is flippant with titles as usual. She is talking about Lord George Hamilton, the Secretary of the India Office, which handles all matters to do with India in England. We wrote to him a few weeks ago, seeking permission to travel to India. A huge party is being organized by the Viceroy of India to celebrate the new King-Emperor Edward VII, or Uncle Bertie, as he is to us. It is called the *durbar* and everyone we know is travelling to attend it. The *durbar* celebrations will be held over twelve days and we are desperate to be there.

Catherine rises to her feet. "He's given us permission?"

Bamba grabs her hands to spin her around before they both collapse on the sofa next to me. I barely get out of the way and end up spilling some of my tea.

"Not quite," Bamba says when she gets her breath back.

"Why are we celebrating then?" I demand, annoyed at the tea stain on my lovely new dress.

Catherine clambers up from the sofa to grab the envelope from the floor. Opening the letter, her eyes scan the words and then she looks up, indignant. "Lord Hamilton is saying we can't go, Bamba!"

"Read it again, dear sister," Bamba replies.

Catherine loses her patience. "Stop the games!"

Bamba sits up straight, suddenly looking very serious. "Old Hamilton says we mustn't attend the *durbar* as there is not enough time left for arrangements to be made that would be fitting for us princesses."

"So we can't go?" Sometimes I really do not understand my big sister.

Bamba shakes her head. "We can't go to the *durbar*. The emphasis is on the event. But he hasn't said that we can't go to India."

The doubt I am feeling is all over Catherine's face. "But—"

"No!" Bamba holds up her hand. "This is how we will interpret the letter. Permission has not been refused. Therefore, in my eyes permission has been granted."

Catherine and I exchange a look. Can we dare it? Can we be that bold? Bamba has already made up her mind for all of us. She gets to her feet and pulls me and Catherine into a group hug.

"Papa couldn't step on ancestral land, but we will. We are going to Punjab. And nobody – and I mean *nobody* – is going to stop us this time."

I do not argue with Bamba. It is quite impossible to do so because she is so headstrong. She is exactly like Papa.

He would often say that his eldest was like his mother, Maharani Jindan. Being headstrong did not do her much good though. Papa told us that his mother had been dragged away screaming from her small son as he was being tricked into handing over his kingdom.

I top up my tea from the pot as Bamba excitedly plans our trip. It has been a long time since I have seen her this happy. Catherine and I have been so concerned for her. She has been low ever since she returned from America.

Bamba wanted to become a doctor, just like Elizabeth Garrett Anderson, the first female doctor in Britain. Mrs Anderson qualified a good few years ago in England, but since then the rules have been changed. It seems one female doctor was one too many for the British Medical Association. They have now banned all women from qualifying as doctors. That is why Bamba had to move to the USA. She enrolled on to a medical course at the Northwestern University near Chicago. Despicably, the university decided halfway through her training to throw all the women students off the course.

Bamba was furious, but there was nothing she could do. She raged at the world, which would not allow her the freedom to be who she wants to be. I do share some of Bamba's sense of injustice. Why can't women train as doctors? Why can't we be who we want to be? Of course, these are useless questions. It is simply the way of the world and men rule it. Change is impossible.

Catherine and I tried extremely hard to lift Bamba's spirits, but nothing worked. The only thing to have brought the sparkle back into her eyes is the thought of visiting India. This trip will be good for her. She has been yearning to see our ancestral land for years.

I shall support her in this rebellion against the wishes of the Empire. Queen Vi is dead. It is not as if I would be hurting my godmother's feelings. As for Uncle Bertie, well, he may have been Papa's best friend, but he is not mine.

Bamba's happiness must come before the feelings of the King-Emperor.

Chapter 10

India at Last

1902–3

I travel separately from Bamba and Catherine. They take a ship from Tilbury Docks and a few days later I follow, with my housekeeper. Our tickets are booked under false names in case the news of our journey reaches the office of Lord Hamilton.

"No man shall treat us like Colonel Hogg treated Papa in Port Said all those years ago," Bamba had said fiercely when she hugged me goodbye. "Remember to keep a low profile on the ship. Don't draw attention to yourself by chatting to strangers. British spies are everywhere, ready to report back to Hamilton."

"I wish we could travel together," Catherine said, dabbing her handkerchief to her eyes. "It doesn't feel right for us to separate."

"Oh for goodness' sake, Cath!" Bamba exploded. Now that she has made up her mind about India, she is petrified that something will go wrong, and we will be caught and stopped by Hamilton. "You know that three Indian women with our description, travelling together, would cause suspicion. The India Office wouldn't even let us get past Gibraltar before hauling us off."

"But, Soph…"

"I'll be fine, Cath," I said reassuringly, hugging my sister. "I'm the one in danger of being recognized because of my pictures in the newspapers. It's better that I travel on my own. Besides, I'll have my housekeeper to keep me company."

"We will meet again in Papa's land," Catherine said bravely.

"We will," I promised.

The first day on the ship reminds me of that trip long ago with my family. Papa was so adamant about his right to return to his homeland and Mama was the opposite, not wanting to offend Queen Vi. Looking back now, I can see why Mama and Papa were so unhappy together. Perhaps Papa fell out of love with Mama because she didn't support his dream. And I also remembered poor Eddie on that trip, as terrified of the water as me. I still miss him.

I make an effort to shake off the sadness. After all, I have far more important things to worry about, like not being reported to Hamilton. It only takes a visit to the dining hall on the second day for me to be recognized. How did I think I could avoid it? I am, after all, one of the most photographed women in England for my fashion sense and society lifestyle. Two English ladies point at me. I refuse to acknowledge them and leave the dining hall. From that day, I take my meals in my cabin and only venture out on to the deck for fresh air late at night, when I know it will be deserted.

I don't know what I'm more terrified of: not reaching India or Bamba's furious reaction if I fail.

The Indian crew on the ship definitely know who I am and are as attentive as they can be. I don't mind them so much. I doubt that their gossip about the British-Indian princess will bring a British officer to my cabin door to order me back to England.

When I finally reach India, I meet up with Bamba and Catherine at a Delhi hotel. All three of us are melting with the Indian heat despite the ceiling fans. We have never experienced anything like it.

"Right, Sophie, now that you've made it, let's make our way to Lahore," Bamba says. "It was our grandfather's capital city."

"We don't know anyone there," Catherine says in a worried voice.

Bamba raises her chin. It is a sign of her defiance. It is the pose she used to adopt whenever English ladies gossiped behind her back, loud enough for her to overhear.

"We are the blood of the Maharaja Ranjit Singh. His followers will welcome us home."

I gaze at my big sister. "Do you really believe that?"

Bamba's expression softens, the anger gone. She places a hand on her heart. "I know it in here."

Chapter 11

The Maharaja's Kingdom

1903

The servant boy's body sways in time with the huge hand-fan clutched between his palms. It is nearly as big as he is, made from yellow straw, its edges decorated by flowers embroidered with what looks like incredibly thick thread. I peep at him through my lashes. The steady motion is making his eyes droop, and I fear that any moment now he will fall to the floor in a deep slumber. And of course, then he will be sacked from his position, as such unprofessionalism will not do in the house of my hosts.

I clear my throat and pointedly look at the fan. It is enough to jolt the boy out of his sleepiness. Suddenly alert, he puts more energy into sweeping the air. I draw my attention back to the others, satisfied that the young boy will not lose his job today.

My sisters and I are in the beautiful city of Lahore. It is filled with palaces and buildings from the time when the Muslim Mughal Empire ruled, before my grandfather. Since the arrival of the British, Christian churches have been added to the city's many other holy buildings: Muslim mosques, Sikh gurdwaras and Hindu mandirs. I never knew this country was home to so many different faiths.

News of our arrival in Lahore travelled fast. In fact it got there before we did. It was Bamba who spotted the welcome party on the station platform. She peered through the window bars (the trains here have bars instead of glass windows) and gasped.

"There are people here with garlands of flowers," she exclaimed.

"There must be someone important on the train." I stood up and smoothed my dress. We had been sitting for hours.

To our absolute delight, the gifts of sweet-smelling flowers were for us. Bamba was right. We were warmly welcomed by the Indian aristocrats who had served under our grandfather. Most welcoming was Umrao Singh and his wife. We call her Sirdarni, which means 'respectful Sikh lady'. Sirdarni's ancestors were imprisoned by the

71

English soldiers for standing with our grandmother Maharani Jindan in her rebellion.

It is in Sirdani's drawing room that the boy is sleepily fanning us.

"So, we are told that the *durbar* in Delhi to welcome the new Emperor-King was quite spectacular," Bamba says in a bitter tone.

Sirdarni rolls her eyes. "Twelve days it lasted, and there were processions of elephants and—"

"Shame old Bertie couldn't be bothered to attend his own celebration," Bamba interrupts.

Sirdarni nearly chokes on her glass of rose sherbert. "Bertie? You mean the King-Emperor?"

"Yes, him." Bamba's tone makes it clear that she does not bow down to anyone.

Sirdarni looks amused. "Do you know him well?"

"He was our papa's best friend until Papa came to his senses about being robbed of his homeland. Bertie was frequently a guest at Elveden House."

"Elveden House?"

"That was what our home was called," Bamba explains. "Still is. It was sold to pay off debts."

"Why do you think Bertie didn't come?" Catherine asks. I know she is changing the subject because she does not want us to go into detail about Papa's enormous debts. The whole of England may very well know about Papa's drinking and gambling habits through the newspapers, but there is no need for Papa's people to know what he was reduced to by the end. Let them continue to think of him tenderly, as that little eight-year-old boy tricked into signing his kingdom away.

Bamba shrugs. "Because Bertie doesn't care for state duties halfway around the world. Anyway, enough about him. Tell me, Sirdarni, how is it that some Indian kings were able to keep their royal positions and our papa was not?"

Sirdarni carefully places her glass down on the perfectly carved wooden table. "They bowed down to the Empire. Your grandmother Maharani Jindan refused. Your papa was a young boy. They tricked a child into signing a treaty. Our elders were there when the English soldiers dragged Maharani Jindan away, screaming. It is all they could talk about for years. A widow and her child were no match for the sly cunning and the military might of the conqueror. We did try to fight for freedom. We tried. Once they removed Maharaja Duleep to England, we knew it was all over. We wanted to survive, so we bowed down to the new rulers. They allowed us to live, but with no power of our own."

"Would Papa have been allowed to remain here if his mother had not fought?" Bamba demanded.

"No." Sirdarni shakes her head. "He would have always been regarded as a rallying point for resistance against the British. He was the descendant of the greatest Sikh maharaja. Men would flock to him and hold him up as a symbol. The royals that have been allowed to remain in their kingdoms today have no real power. They are puppets of the Empire. Sadly, there is no royal man left in this entire subcontinent who can inspire resistance."

"There may be no royal figure," Bamba says, "but there must be others who are ready to rebel and lead."

Sirdani nods. "There are, but it is dangerous to talk and the walls have ears."

I glance at the small boy whose eyes are drooping again. Could he be a spy for the British? Is he paid to provide information on what goes inside the homes of the aristocratic Indians? Is there no place in this world safe from British spies?

Over the next few days I become friendly with the fan boy, even though I still entertained random thoughts of him being a spy. I decide he can't possibly be one and remove the idea firmly from my mind. His name is Pawan.

I want to experience the real India outside the palaces and ask Pawan to show me his home. It is one of a collection of mud huts far from Sirdani's estate. I bend my head as I enter his home, which seems to consist of just one room. He has two younger sisters who gaze up at me with big eyes. His mother looks overwhelmed that I have set foot in her home. She clutches her dupatta, a type of shawl, to her mouth and ogles me. I don't stay long. Pawan takes me on a tour of his village and the inhabitants come out to gawk at me. They can't quite believe the granddaughter of their dead Maharaja Ranjit Singh is walking amongst them.

Later that evening after dinner, I tell Bamba about my day trip.

"Do you think it's like this in all of India?" I ask.

She nods. "Big gaps between the rich and poor are everywhere."

"But not so much in England..."

"Soph!" Bamba darts an annoyed look at me. "It's just the same in England. When have you ever ventured out of the rich parts of London to see how the poor live?"

"I—"

"You've been mollycoddled. You have no idea how the poor live. Why should you? You're surrounded by your horses and dogs, living a life of luxury in the grounds of Hampton Court Palace."

"Bamba…" I feel hurt by her words and try to say something to defend myself but no words emerge.

Bamba sighs and sits back. "It's not your fault, Soph. You've been protected."

I find my voice. "You were really mean to me just now, Bamba."

"Telling the truth is not being mean. You should see life for what it really is."

"But—"

"Do you know Papa wasn't the selfish big spender that the newspapers made him out to be?" she suddenly says. "He helped the unfortunate in his own way."

"He did?"

Bamba nodded. "When Papa was eighteen years old, he noticed the plight of the lascars in England. He was shocked at their treatment by British sea captains who employed them in India to work on their ships, then dumped them in British ports with no money or any way to return home. So Papa built the 'The Strangers Home', which was a home for lascars in the West India Dock Road, in London. I have heard that Albert even laid the first stone at Papa's request. Albert had a lot of affection for Papa."

"You mean Queen Vi's husband, Prince Albert?" Typically, Bamba doesn't bother with titles.

"Yes, him."

"I didn't know about any of this."

Bamba doesn't seem to hear me. Instead, a scowl covers her face. "I hate it that some people view Papa as a failure for not being able to take back Punjab. He was one man against a mighty empire."

"He was," I agree, wondering where this conversation is going.

"I don't think big achievements are the only things that people should be remembered for. Papa made a difference to the lives of extremely poor men who were cold, hungry and stranded in a strange country."

Bamba is in the mood for ranting, which means something has triggered her. I walk over and place my arm around my big sister. "Has something happened to upset you?"

Her eyes fill with tears and she blinks them back, furious at what she considers to be the sign of weakness.

"Bamba." I hug her tightly. "Tell me."

She disentangles herself from my arms and bites her lip. Finally she says, "I just wish Papa had realized his dream. It's hard for me to take pleasure in all that is wonderful here, knowing that Papa was denied it."

"You feel guilty?"

She nods. "I guess I do."

"He would want us to be happy," I say. "He couldn't make it here but we did. Let us enjoy his kingdom in his name."

Bamba manages a wonky smile through the tears. "In his name."

Chapter 12

Heaven's Fruit

1903

We are standing in the shade of trees, beautiful green trees with blobs of orange and yellow hanging from their branches.

It is finally the season of the mango and Sirdani arranges a trip to the orchard for us. I had mentioned my fascination with the fruit to her once and she promised that I would taste a mango before I returned home to England.

I shield my eyes from the sun to squint up at the nearest tree. Pawan has accompanied us and has already climbed halfway up. His bare feet are balanced on a branch, and his arms are high above his head, shaking the branch above. The mangoes fall to the ground.

Bamba leans down to pick one up. It fits into the palm of her hand and she squeezes it. "So this is what Queen Vi pined for?"

I say nothing. In the carriage ride from Sirdani's house to the orchard, I told my sisters about that long-ago conversation in Buckingham Palace with Queen Vi and her Munshi-ji, Abdul Karim. The one about Queen Vi's desire for mangoes.

I crouch down and wonder how to select the best fruit – the one that promises to taste like heaven, in the words of Munshi-ji. Reaching forward, I curve my palm around the nearest one. The skin is thick and smooth and reminds me of banana peel. I squeeze it and the mango dents slightly. The flesh inside must be soft.

"Is it like a peach?" Catherine calls out to Pawan.

He looks down at her. "What?" He doesn't know what 'peach' means and we don't know the Indian word for it.

"Never mind," Catherine says.

"Are we supposed to bite the skin?" Bamba licks a spot and immediately regrets it. "Yuck."

Pawan stares at us as if we are mad and then grins.

"He's going to be telling the story of the three princesses of Punjab and how they didn't know how to eat a mango, isn't he?" Catherine says drily.

"Show us then," Bamba snaps impatiently, once again the demanding princess, expecting others to fall in line.

Pawan's grin disappears as he recognizes the authority. He climbs down from the tree and reaches into his back pocket to retrieve a penknife. Then he drops down, picks up the mango closest to his feet and slices into the skin. I watch, fascinated, as he holds up gleaming yellow flesh.

"Will it taste like a banana or an apple?" I ask.

Pawan doesn't offer the slice to us. Instead, he raises the fruit to his mouth and scrapes the flesh with his teeth. Juice trickles down the side of his mouth.

Catherine looks a little appalled at the messiness of it all, but Bamba grabs the knife and cuts into her own mango. Then she takes a bite. Her eyes widen. "Oh my word," she mumbles through a mouthful. "This is delicious."

It's my turn to grab the knife and in my haste, I squeeze the mango as I cut it. The juice spills out onto my fingers. They feel sticky. I don't care and pop the fruit in my mouth.

Oh my goodness!

I have never tasted anything so sweet, so tender and so mouth-watering.

"Or you could eat it like this," Pawan says, peeling the skin off with his fingers and biting into the flesh as if it were an apple. Juice stains his lips and trickles down the sides of his mouth. Bamba and I wrench the skin off our own mangoes and attack the flesh.

"Come on, Cath," Bamba says. "You don't know what you're missing."

Catherine accepts a peeled mango from Bamba and takes a small, ladylike bite. That's all it takes to convince her to abandon her dignified ways. Within seconds, she is sitting cross-legged on the ground, devouring the heavenly fruit with me, Bamba and Pawan.

I can't help thinking of Queen Vi when I bite into my third mango. She would have loved them and it is a shame that she never got to taste one.

Chapter 13

Sailing Home

1903

Nine months later, I think it is time to go home.

I have loved being in India, but I yearn for England. I miss my dogs, my horses and my friends. But I know I will be returning with a change in my heart. The poverty in these lands is so heartbreaking. There is so much for so few, whilst so many remain hungry or even starve. Queen Vi used to say that everything is as it should be. I am not so sure about that any more.

There are some men in India today who want the British to leave. Just like Papa did. They claim that the British have no right to rule over the Indian people. They talk about freedom.

Perhaps Papa was ahead of his time.

Perhaps it was freedom he was fighting for.

Bamba told me about the American struggle for independence against the British only about a hundred years ago. We weren't taught this history in school, but Bamba became aware of it from her time at medical college, brief though it was.

"The USA used to be a British colony much like India," Bamba told me. "The Americans objected to being ruled by Britain and revolted. They have been free of the British since 1783."

Maybe the Indians' determination to win their independence is the same as the Americans'. I wish them luck with their movement.

I know this much. This land, India, may be part of my heritage, but it is not my home.

England is. I'm going home.

I say goodbye to Bamba. She is incredibly upset that I am leaving. I do not think she understands how I can view England as home after everything we have learned about our family. India is now home for Bamba. I do not think she will ever return to England. And I can't blame her for not wanting to. She is our father's daughter. She is his true heir, his *sherni*.

The voyage to England will take four weeks. I am glad of the opportunity to have some time to myself. Time to think. It seems to me that I am no longer the pampered princess who travelled to India. I am returning as a woman who has seen how the other half live. The poverty in India is shocking and I wish I could do more to help. I never thought people could exist like that. It makes my own existence of parties and dog shows seem quite vain. I feel as if I have turned a corner. I want my life to count for something. I cannot while it away on frivolous things.

For the first time in my life, I am intrigued by the history between India and Britain. How did the British manage to conquer a sprawling sub-continent? As luck would have it, I become friendly with a British-Indian gentleman on the journey home. He is full of knowledge and I look forward to our daily chats on the deck before dinner.

Professor Kumar is an academic who was raised and educated in London. He is tall with perfect hair and manners, like many of the rich Indians living in England. He teaches at University College, London and is especially interested in history.

One evening, we are standing by the railing breathing in the fresh sea air. An Indian crewman, a lascar, is sweeping the deck further down. He glances towards us and I realize he wants to clean this end but dares not disturb us. I wave at him.

"It's all right," I call. "We won't get in your way."

He freezes for a second before recovering. Professor Kumar and I walk over to the deckchairs lined against the wall. Sitting down, we watch as the lascar performs his task.

"What's your name?" I call to him.

He looks shocked to be addressed directly.

"She asked for your name," Professor Kumar says gently.

"Raju," he replies nervously.

I smile. "Where are you from?"

"Rajasthan."

"Ah, I see," I say. "Not far from Punjab."

"Yes, Princess-ji."

His answer surprises me. "You know who I am?"

"Every Indian on this ship knows that the granddaughter of the great Maharaja Ranjit Singh is travelling amongst them."

I cannot help blushing. I am used to being noticed, but all my life it was because I was a god-daughter to Queen Victoria, not because of who my grandfather was.

Raju suddenly bows. "It is an honour to be in the company of an Indian princess."

I nod and smile, unsure what to say. Raju returns to his task and soon Professor Kumar and I are left to ourselves.

"What do you know about these lascars?" I suddenly ask, wanting to know more about the men that my papa helped.

"They are poor labourers who sought employment," Professor Kumar says. "Thousands of them now work on British ships. They are reliable workers and do not drink alcohol. With a lascar crew, there are no problems of drunkenness on board, and they are cheaper than English sailors."

"Cheaper? You mean they are paid less? How is that right?"

"There are many things in the world that are not right," Professor Kumar says.

I ask the question that has nagged me since Bamba told me about how Papa helped them. "Why are they called lascars? Do you know?"

"Portuguese seamen used this name for the Indian sailors they employed. The word originally meant 'soldier' in Persian."

"Really? But why are they still called lascars, rather than sailors?"

Professor Kumar shrugs. "The word just stuck. It's

because the Portuguese were the first Europeans to rediscover India."

"Rediscover?"

"Yes, India wasn't 'discovered' by Europeans in the fifteenth century, like America was. There has always been trade between Asia and Europe. The ancient Greek king, Alexander the Great, conquered the north-west of India, in 327 BCE."

I blink. "That's three hundred years before the birth of Jesus."

The Professor chuckles. "Yes, a long time before your grandfather made Punjab his kingdom."

"Oh."

"We think the Vikings also knew about our country. Archaeological finds show that coins and beads from India were brought to England."

"Oh, I didn't know about that," I admit. "My governess only taught me that the Vikings were terrible conquerors who came to England to pillage and steal."

Professor Kumar gives me a dry smile. "Isn't that always how the conquered view their conquerors?"

He sounds like Bamba now. I change the subject. "What were you saying about the Portuguese?"

"Well, in 1498, a Portuguese explorer sailed all the

way to south India. His name was Vasco de Gama and he restarted trade between the two continents after a pause of several hundred years. Then the Spanish followed."

"Isn't that interesting?" I say. "I always thought the English were first."

"No, they were behind the other two nations, which at the time were more powerful, so the English had to play catch-up very quickly."

"How?"

"Queen Elizabeth's navy defeated the Spanish fleet, called the Armada, and grabbed all its surviving ships. That was the start of real English naval power. I am sorry, I'm teaching you rather than having a conversation. It is one of the perils of being an academic."

"No," I protest. "I'm interested. Please tell me more."

"Well, in December 1600, a group of English merchants went to see Queen Elizabeth. They informed her that they wished to engage in international trade, just like Portugal and Spain. They painted a picture of all the riches they could bring back to England and Elizabeth was intrigued. She asked them what they required from her."

"Well, what did they need?" I ask, intrigued myself.

"Just paperwork with her signature, declaring that she had granted permission for the merchants to trade in her name. Elizabeth didn't want England to fall behind the other European powers who were exploring new lands and claiming them as their own. She signed the papers, which they called a Trade Licence, and wished her merchants good luck.

"The following year, the merchants' first ship docked in the spice islands of Indonesia. The journey to India followed in 1608. These merchants called themselves the Company of Merchants of London Trading into the East Indies. They later shortened the name to the English East India Company."

"I did not know that."

"The venture was initially just about the spice trade," he explains. "On that first voyage, the ship returned to England with 500 tonnes of green peppercorns. Later, the Company started trading in cotton and silk and became so successful that it even set up its own private army in India to protect its interests. Slowly, its power grew and with it, so did the greed and ambition of the Company's directors. By the mid-1700s, they decided to take over Indian land and overthrow Indian rulers. Local Indians were forced to pay taxes to the Company. You can rule anyone when you have your own army of soldiers, fully armed with weapons."

"And then what happened?" I ask, even though I know from my own family history.

"The Company was just about profit. It expanded and expanded, swallowing large chunks of Indian land. After the death of your grandfather, his throne was inherited by his son Duleep, who was still a small child. The Company sniffed out weakness and made its move on Punjab. It would never have dared while Maharaja Ranjit Singh was alive, for he would have defended his kingdom and sent the Company packing with its tail between its legs. So they bided their time and finally made their move once the old Maharaja was gone. Duleep was a young boy with only his mother to defend him."

I lean my head back in my chair to gaze up at the sky. "And those Indian royals who rebelled, like my grandmother Maharani Jindan, lost their kingdoms, while those who bowed down became the puppets of the new British rulers."

"Something like that."

I think of those Indian rajas and nawabs who got to keep their titles and remain on their ancestral land. The ones who entertained my sisters and me in their palaces, and who attended the Viceroy's *durbar* while we were kept out. We, the granddaughters of the greatest Sikh king that ever ruled Punjab.

"Apart from my grandmother, who were the other rulers who rebelled against the East India Company?"

"There were many," he admits. "One of the most famous is Tipu Sultan, the Great Tiger of Mysore. Betrayed by his own side and defeated in battle."

I roll the betrayed king's name on my tongue. "Tipu Sultan."

"There was a famous queen defeated only recently."

"Queen?"

"Laxmi Bai, the queen of Jhansi. Killed."

"A queen?" I repeat.

"It was Laxmi Bai and her friends that actually ended the Company's power."

I sit up. "How?"

"In 1857, Indian rebels rose up against Company rule and hundreds died. They call it the Indian Mutiny. The British government was not pleased with the way the Company handled the rebellion, so they dissolved it. Everything the Company owned – from land to soldiers – was confiscated by the Crown. This is when your godmother, Queen Victoria, became the Empress of India. The British government now directly rules India, rather than the English East India Company."

I sigh heavily. I don't want to talk about the Empire

any more. I want to change the subject back to the lascars, so I tell him about Papa's charity work. The professor is so knowledgeable that I suspect he will be aware of Papa's final years of struggle. I want him to think of Papa as more than the man he became in the end. And so I tell him about Papa's work in funding the Oriental Seaman refuge for the lascars.

Professor Kumar politely listens before looking impressed. "Your papa did a good thing and probably saved the lives of countless men."

I nod, suddenly feeling really proud of Papa. It is a part of him that I never knew, and I can't help thinking that perhaps that was the man that Mama fell in love with all those years ago. And then it hits me. Maybe I could follow in Papa's footsteps and continue his work.

"I think I shall take up Papa's cause to help the lascars," I suddenly say, surprising myself. "I have seen them on the London docks, cold and shivering. I shall help them."

"How will you do that?"

I smile. "I have extraordinarily rich friends. I shall fundraise to build a new lascar house for those in need."

Professor Kumar stands and offers me his arm. "Come, Princess, let us go to dinner. These things are the way of the world and you shouldn't worry your pretty little head about them."

Suddenly I feel dejected and can only manage the smallest of false smiles. Professor Kumar had spoiled our conversation with that last line. I wish Bamba were here so she could tell him where to stick his opinions about pretty little heads. I, ever the diplomatic sister, say nothing and rise to my feet to take his arm. I don't need his permission or approval to care about people or to help the lascars. I will do it anyway.

Chapter 14

A Suffragette

1908

I have been invited to stay at a friend's house in Warwickshire. I was reluctant to accept the invitation at first, as I am not feeling very sociable at the moment. The years have sped by. Nowadays, I find the London season quite dull. Everything feels like repetition. Same parties, same people, same talk. There is nothing new. Nothing to excite me. Nothing to feel passionate about any more, especially now that the lascar home is complete.

My project to help the lascars on my return from India was successful and thousands walk through the door of the new home every year. With donations raised from all my rich London friends, I have built a lascar boarding house in London's Victoria Docks. Papa's original lascar home in east London's West India Dock Road had been badly in need of repair, so I chose a brand-new location for the new home. If a lascar loses his job or has little money, he has a place to go, where people are dedicated to helping him. There is shelter and food provided for those far away from home, just like Papa intended.

I think Papa would be proud of me if he were alive today.

Freddie, Victor and Anne congratulated me at the launch party of the new home. I basked in their pride, even though I was really disappointed that Bamba and Catherine couldn't be there, too.

Bamba has point-blank refused to return to England. To the dismay of the Viceroy, she has purchased a bungalow and named it 'The Palms' in Lahore and is now calling herself the Princess of Punjab.

Her letters to me are filled with names and descriptions of Sikh men. She is trying to play matchmaker to tempt me back to India for romance. Her letters do make me laugh though, especially her attempts at drawing. My big sister is a lot of things, but an artist she is not. Her hand-drawn pictures of these Sikh suitors are terrible and I'm sure they do no justice to the poor men at all.

I think Bamba will settle down soon with a Sikh man. She has already converted back to Sikhism. Truly, she is Papa's heir.

Catherine, my sweet sister Catherine, is now living in Germany with her friend Lina Schaeffer. Lina was Catherine and Bamba's governess at one time. Catherine is happy there and I am glad for her. I would rather she were here with me, but we are all grown-ups now and must lead our own lives. Only, I do not feel I am living much of a life.

When I complain to Bamba in my letters, she writes back jokingly that pampered princesses are not allowed to be bored. I think the joke is on me. I need something new in my life. Something to make me want to fling back my bedcovers and face the day with enthusiasm. I used to feel like that about my dog shows and horse races, but I just can't muster up the joy. Hardly surprising really, as joy should be instinctive rather than something we have to muster.

In my last letter to Catherine, I even admitted to feeling lonely. Unlike my sisters, I have not found fulfilment in other countries. England is still my home, and I suspect it always will be. I do not want to be anywhere else. But I feel at a loss when it comes to filling my days. My friends tell me that I must socialize. Get out and about and feel the fresh air. And so, I have accepted this invitation and here I am in Warwickshire.

The country air is indeed wonderful and for the first time in a while, I am in a gathering with new people.

On the first evening, we are sitting in the ladies' room after dinner whilst the men withdraw for their cigars. Out hostess has given a young woman permission to say a few words. She looks to be about my age and has taken a position by the fireplace. I cannot help noticing her white dress, which is trimmed with purple and green. It is not very fashionable at all to wear a combination of such colours, and I am left wondering who her clothes designer is. I make a mental note to recommend my own dressmakers to her. It is the only polite thing to do.

I sit back in my chair, intrigued to hear what the woman has to say. I would never have the confidence to command a room like this. My voice would simply tremble with nerves.

"Ladies," she begins in an assured voice. "My name is Una Dugdale and I am a suffragette."

I sneak a look at the other ladies in the room. Two have gasped aloud, but the rest seem to be just as nonplussed as me. What on earth is a suffragette? Una seems to be aware of the naivety in the room because she smiles and says, "Let me explain."

I lean forward, suddenly very curious.

"I am a member of the Women's Social and Political

Union. You might have heard us called the WSPU. It was founded in the north of England by Mrs Emmeline Pankhurst and her daughters, Christabel and Sylvia. We are a women-only political organization campaigning for women's suffrage in the United Kingdom. We are the suffragettes and we have only one aim – the right for women to have the vote."

I am suddenly aware that my mouth has fallen open like a fish. I quickly close it so that I don't appear unladylike. Una's words are quite bewildering. Women to have the right to vote! Who ever heard of such a thing? I certainly hadn't.

"Yes, you heard that correctly," Una announces, one hand on her hip, looking very much like a male politician addressing a rally of supporters. Except I do not know how many supporters Una has in the room, because some of the other guests look quite shocked.

"We women should be given the right to decide who gets to be in power." Una's voice is higher now and she is waving a fist in the air. "Why shouldn't we have a say in who gets to make the laws that we must all obey? Are we not human?"

Her last question is like a punch to my stomach. It is so basic. Of course we women are human. And yet, she is right. We do not have the same rights as men. This is something so simple and yet so complicated at the same time. I can't tear my eyes away from Una. I have never met anybody so extraordinary, and I soak up every word that comes out of her mouth.

"Two years ago, we began demonstrations outside Parliament. Some of us were arrested. Some were imprisoned. We did not break. We will not break. We wear these colours – purple, green and white – to symbolize our struggle. Mrs Pankhurst says the purple stands for loyalty and dignity, white stands for purity in private and public, and green is the colour of hope, of spring."

Ah. So the colours of her dress that I dismissed as unfashionable actually stand for something.

"Votes for women!" Una bellows, fist in the air.

As if in a trance, I rise to my feet and clap loudly. A few of the other women join me, but the remaining guests stay seated, looking unimpressed.

Una's gaze turns to me and she smiles slightly. Believing her speech to be over, I walk up and extend my hand shyly. "Sophia Singh."

Her smile widens. "I know who you are, Princess."

The acknowledgement makes me flush. I am flattered that someone like her knows who I am. "That was quite a wonderful speech," I gush. "You had such passion in your words."

"Thank you, dear Princess."

"We women really do not have the same rights as men," I say. "I thought of my poor sister Bamba and her dashed hopes of becoming a doctor."

"Tell me," Una encourages me.

I explain how Bamba had travelled to America in order to get the qualification she wasn't allowed to study for here in England, only to be thrown off the medical course halfway through.

"All because some of the men objected to the women's presence," I finish my story with a sigh.

Una shakes her head. "Barbaric."

"Bamba didn't deserve that," I say sadly. "She would have made a wonderful doctor and the profession would have given her what she has been searching for all her life."

"And what's that?"

"Meaning," I say.

Una nods. "No doubt we women have been searching for meaning for most of our lives. That, and purpose."

"Yes! It would have given Bamba's life a purpose."

"Perhaps you would like to join me at our next meeting in London?"

I do not need to be asked again. I link my arm through Una's, and we begin to stroll around the large drawing room. "Tell me more."

Princess Bamba Duleep Singh
Lahore, Punjab
India

1908
Dear Bamba,

You will not believe what I have been doing. I have joined the Women's Social and Political Union. I am campaigning to get women the vote!

Isn't it marvellous? I have joined my local branch, which is based in Richmond and Kingston upon Thames. It is wonderful to make all these new friends from all walks of life. Although we are so different from each other, we are united in our cause. It is good to be part of something. Some of that loneliness and boredom I spoke of before has somewhat reduced.

I offered my services at the branch and they asked me what I was good at. I didn't think 'dogs, horses and clothes' would really be a fitting answer, so I mentioned my charity work for the lascars' home.

They said fundraising would be really useful, so I have been baking cakes and making jam. Well, let me rephrase that. My cook has been baking cakes and making jam, and I've been taking all the treats to the bazaars and selling them. I tell you, my princess cakes are gone within minutes. All bought and gobbled up.

I have also been asked to recruit other women from my own circle. My new friend Una thinks some of the women only come to see a princess rather than to hear about the cause of women's suffrage. I know! I know! You're probably stomping around the garden right now saying, "I told you so! They think we're exotic birds."

Una says it is not because I am of Indian heritage, but because I am a princess. I do suspect that she may be right. After all, London is home to many thousands of Indians. The city is filled with Indian royals, current and dispossessed, as well as lawyers, businessmen and students. There are even lascars for the lower classes to gawp at.

Bamba, I think Una is right. The fascination is not with our skin colour. It is with our royal birth and status, and I fully intend to take advantage of it to help the sisterhood.

Also, please stop sending me pictures of men. I am not interested in returning to India to live.

With all my love,

Soph

Chapter 15

Meeting Emmeline

1908

"This way," Una says, leading me from the front door into the large, central-London house. "She is in here."

I take a deep breath as I follow my friend. I have been nervous all morning, waiting for this hour. A few days ago, Una informed me that the leader of the WSPU, Mrs Emmeline Pankhurst, had expressed a desire to meet me. Of course, I immediately said yes and then the nerves set in. Mrs Pankhurst is a woman unafraid to challenge the highest office in the land for what she believes in, and she comes with a fierce reputation. Determined not to make a fool of myself by appearing uninformed, I made a point to find out as much as I could about her. It wasn't very hard. So far, I have found out that she was born Emmeline Goulden in Manchester in 1858, the eldest of ten children.

Her parents were politically active and they encouraged her from a young age to be so as well. They campaigned against slavery and were supporters of female suffrage.

That bit was complete news to me. I had no idea that there had been a movement for women's suffrage since 1872, when the National Society for Women's Suffrage was set up. It seems I have been living in my own little world of dogs, horses and balls.

Emmeline married Dr Richard Pankhurst and campaigned for him to be elected to Parliament, although he was never successful. I suspect it was because his views of equality between men and women must have seemed too radical to the people in charge of the country. After he died, Emmeline set up the WSPU in 1903 with the slogan 'Deeds not words'.

Mrs Pankhurst does not believe that simply asking for our right to vote will get us what we want. She believes that action must be taken.

"Through here," Una says, turning the door handle.

Butterflies suddenly begin to flutter in my stomach. It is unusual for me to feel this way about another person. I have been in the company of empresses and queens, but none have made me as nervous as the leader of the suffragettes. This woman's reputation is her own, forged by her own actions, rather than by birth or marriage. Her own activism is what makes her so inspiring.

I step inside a large room and my gaze falls on a rather gaunt-looking woman seated on a sofa. She rises to her feet to walk towards us, dressed in a high-collared white blouse and black skirt. Her hair is piled on top of her head and her face is somewhat lined. I can't help thinking that her life's work shows on her face. The worry, the tension and her struggle are all there, and it gives her an air of aloofness.

"Emmeline," says Una. "May I introduce Princess Sophia Duleep Singh?"

Mrs Pankhurst's smile transforms her face and she suddenly appears more approachable. "Nice to meet you, Princess Sophia."

"Just Sophia," I squeak. "Please just call me Sophia."

"Sophia," she repeats in a gentler tone. I think she has guessed that I feel a little intimidated, so she tries to put me at ease. "And you must call me Emmeline."

She leads us to the sofa and the three of us sit down.

"I have heard a lot about the god-daughter of Queen Victoria," Emmeline says. "It fills me with joy to know that you have been working extremely hard to fundraise for us. Not to mention that you've also been hosting parties at your home to invite new women to the cause."

I feel the heat in my cheeks as they redden with the compliment.

"Did you know that Queen Victoria called the fight for women's rights 'a mad, wicked folly'?" she asks me.

I shake my head. I did not know that, but I am not surprised.

Emmeline leans forward so that she can take my hand into hers. "Your support is most welcome and needed," she says. "Our cause will benefit from a name such as yours."

I know that I must emerge from my dazed infatuation. It is as if I have reverted to being the shy, quiet girl of my childhood. The one that was always likened to her shy, quiet mother. Straightening my back, I draw a long, steadying breath. "I will do all I can to help."

"Thank you." Emmeline lets go of my hand and turns to Una. "I think we could do with some tea."

"That sounds lovely," Una agrees, darting an amused look at me. She knows how absolutely star-struck I am.

Emmeline rings her little bell, and a maid pops her head around the door. "A tray for three please," she instructs.

The door closes and we sit in awkward silence. I am too tongue-tied to attempt a conversation. Una finally takes pity on me.

"Sophia has raised funds to build a new house for the

lascars living on the London docks," she says. "There is much exploitation of these poor, brown men."

"That is wonderful," Emmeline says approvingly.

I think back to the information I researched. "I read that you were a Poor Law guardian before you set up the WSPU," I say in a timid voice.

The Poor Law guardians are responsible for the people in poverty who must live in workhouses to survive. I have heard such terrible things about these places, which were originally set up to house and employ men, women and children. The list of abuses is quite horrific and includes forcing very young children to work, and extremely long working hours for the adults. Many workhouse residents don't receive enough food and suffer frequent beatings.

"Ah yes, the first time I went into the place I was horrified to see little girls of seven and eight years old on their knees, scrubbing the cold stones of the long corridors," Emmeline reveals in a sad voice. "Bronchitis was epidemic among them most of the time. I found that there were pregnant women in that workhouse, scrubbing floors, doing the hardest kind of work, almost until their babies came into the world."

"How awful," I mumble.

"The women used to tell me their stories, dreadful

stories some of them," she says, shaking her head. "The condition of women's lives is so deplorable that it is our duty to break the law to call attention to the reasons for this. We must fight for not only ourselves, but for those women who are too poor and too oppressed to do so themselves. It is not right that we have no say in the way our lives are run. In the opportunities given to us. My parents were very politically active, and they allowed me an insight into campaigning for change. And yet I, their daughter, was denied the education that my brothers received. One rule for the boys and another for the girls. That is not equality."

I think of poor Bamba who was thrown off her medical course. She would have liked Emmeline.

"Promise me, Sophia," Emmeline says, taking my hand again. "Promise me that you will commit yourself to this cause for the sisterhood. That you will help us become lawmakers."

"I will," I vow.

"Promise that you will not shy away from the challenges and the danger that will come," Emmeline says. "That you will not abandon the sisterhood for fear of being shunned by the establishment and the circles you move in."

I can barely speak through my captivation with this woman who is fighting for all women.

"Remember this, Sophia," she says. "We wear no mask. We belong to every class. We permeate every class of the country from the highest to the lowest. So, you see, the women's civil war is absolutely impossible for those in power to deal with. You cannot locate it and you cannot stop it. In our struggle, we have tried to be womanly. We have tried feminine influence and we have seen that it is of no use. They have to choose between giving us freedom or giving us death."

I know now that I will not rest until we women are given the vote.

Chapter 16

Black Friday

1910

"The Home Secretary, Mr Winston Churchill, may very well have me arrested today," Emmeline says as we walk together. In step with us is Elizabeth Garrett Anderson, the pioneering doctor in whose footsteps Bamba tried to follow.

I wish Bamba were here to see this, but I know she is happy in India.

"But there will be no truce!" Emmeline repeats again and again with every step.

We are leading a march of three hundred women to the Houses of Parliament because we have been betrayed by the prime minister, Herbert Asquith. During the last general election, Asquith made a campaign promise that he would permit the vote to some women. Not to all women, but it was at least a start. And now he is going back on that promise. Emmeline is furious, as we all are.

By midday we are standing in Parliament Square, bold and loud and making our presence felt. I glance around at the gathered women, my sisters, and wonder if Mr Churchill really will have Emmeline arrested rather than allow her to enter the Houses of Parliament to confront the Prime Minister. I stand by Emmeline's side, ready to defend her, when suddenly, I'm aware that something is happening elsewhere. I can hear screams drifting towards us from the back of the crowd. I throw a quick glance at Emmeline who has paled considerably. We knew there was a chance of arrests, but we were not expecting screaming. Things have suddenly gone so very wrong. The crowd surges towards us. We stumble back and then, out of nowhere, a line of policemen appears. They pin us back against the gates of Parliament. I can barely breathe as I am trapped between the metal gates at my back and these large policemen in front.

Then chaos erupts.

My eyes cannot take in the sight in front of me. Our women and girls are being attacked by the police! A woman younger than me has her blouse ripped. Her corset is visible! She tries to cover herself, but the policeman holds her arms up. The scandal! I cannot believe the policemen's violence! I want to reach out to the poor girl as she screams.

"Get off her!" Emmeline yells.

My vision is blocked by a burly policeman. I cannot see who Emmeline is trying to protect from her own pinned spot, but she looks furious. "Get off her, you oaf!"

It gets worse. The policemen are now tossing the women between them like rag dolls. They are actually hurling them from one man to the next. I have never seen anything quite like it. More screams. There are horses now, charging at the groups of huddled women who are trying to protect themselves from the men. And now it's not just the policemen. Male onlookers have joined the abuse, and some are punching and slapping the women.

Emmeline's voice is hoarse from screaming. "Arrest us if you must, but stop the violence."

One of the policemen pinning us to the gate snorts at her. "Mr Winston Churchill doesn't want any of you filling the cells. We're to use any means necessary to stop you from entering Parliament."

"He has commanded this?" Emmeline shrieks. "What an absolutely horrid man. How can he sit in government and order this violence? It is unacceptable."

"We're just following orders!" The policeman barks

before falling backwards. Something has happened to break the police line.

Oh, bless her! A suffragette is riding a horse against the policemen and some end up on the ground from her charge. It does not last very long, and she is soon pulled off her horse. Her action, however, has led to the police line being broken, giving Emmeline and me the chance to get past the policemen. We both launch ourselves into the crowd to help the women still being attacked.

I rush to a woman who is being choked on the ground. Aiming kicks at the policeman's side, I scream at him to let her go. He glances up at me and then releases the woman. She struggles for breath. For a second I think he is going to punch me in the face. For some reason, he resists the urge. Is it my brown face? Have the police been instructed not to touch the Indian princess for fear of the newspapers printing a photo of me looking all bruised? I do not know why, but the man disappears into the crowd. Once his poor victim is back on her feet, I hurl myself at another man whose hands are all over a young woman.

"Let her go!" I scream.

He pushes me back into the crowd with such force that I almost topple over. On and on it continues. It is never-ending, and I fear that we will all die here. Beaten and trampled. After six long hours, the men's violence finally stops. My hands are locked together in handcuffs and I am hurled with considerable force into the back of the police cart.

I am to be charged with obstructing the police and will have to appear at Bow Street Magistrates' Court in the morning. My elation at being taken seriously by the police is tempered with the shock I still feel at their violence. And then that small burst of triumph is quickly vanquished by Mr Churchill's decision to drop all charges against all the women.

"They don't want the judges to hear testimonies of the police violence," Emmeline says at our hastily called meeting. "They have robbed us of our day in court."

"I'm surprised some of the women weren't killed on the day," I remark, staring down at the front cover of the *Daily Mirror*. The newspaper has published a picture of a suffragette lying semi-conscious on the ground with the shadow of a policeman over her.

We are going to call that disgraceful day of police brutality 'Black Friday'.

Chapter 17

The Prime Minister's Car

1911

Today is 6 February. It is the day of the King's Speech.

The new King.

Uncle Bertie died on 6 May 1910 and his son, George V, is the new King-Emperor.

George V will ride from Buckingham Palace to the Houses of Parliament to deliver his speech about the government's plans for the year. It is going to be a grand ceremonial day. The Horse Guards will march behind the King's carriage along Whitehall. This pomp and ceremony is what the monarchy is so good at and I am going to be a part of it.

"Are you off to Parliament, ma'am?" my maid asks as she helps me dress. I am wearing my white gown and a purple sash with the words 'Votes for Women' emblazoned across it.

"Sort of," I say mischievously.

Within the hour, I am amongst the spectators in Whitehall outside the gates of 10 Downing Street, the Prime Minister's residence. There are butterflies in my stomach in anticipation of what I am about to do, but I try to keep my face as serene as possible. I must not raise any suspicion. I have removed my sash as it will be a giveaway and am wearing only my white dress, a hat and a fur muff. My fingers clutch the poster I have hidden inside my muff. Any minute now the prime minister, Mr Asquith, should emerge from behind the black door to get into his car. The distance from Downing Street to Parliament is not very far at all, but the Prime Minster will be driven there. Where is he? I stretch my neck to see if I can catch a glimpse of Big Ben a short distance away, but the clock face is concealed by the buildings in between.

"He'll be out at any minute now, miss," the policeman at the gate says with a wink.

I am startled that he has noticed my impatience. I suppose it is his job to observe. His gaze, however, is not suspicious and for that I am grateful. I steady my breathing and respond lightly.

"I do hope so. It's a very cold morning."

"Couldn't you get a seat in the public gallery in Parliament, miss?"

I could have. I just chose not to. What is the point of listening to the King read out the new laws that his government propose to pass this year, when not a single woman has had any involvement in the drafting of these laws? I say none of this of course and instead, with a smile on my face, say, "Tickets were gone by the time I applied."

He nods and then his attention is diverted as photographers scuttle forward. The door of Number 10 opens and Mr Asquith emerges. He pauses for a moment so his picture can be taken by the group of photographers, then climbs into his car. The engine is already running and, as soon as the doors shut, the car glides smoothly forward.

This is it.

I pull out the poster from inside my muff.

It reads: 'Give Women the Vote'.

Pushing myself forward from the crowd, I throw myself on to the Prime Minister's car window.

"Votes for women!" I scream, pressing my body against the metal and glass.

The car brakes. The crowd mills around the vehicle. Although they do not have anything to shout about or posters to display, they look caught up in the moment. I am grateful to them as it gives me a few extra seconds to shout at the Prime Minister.

"Votes for women!"

Mr Asquith glares back at me through the window. He looks appalled at my behaviour.

"Sophia Singh," he mouths, shaking his head.

Ha! He recognizes me. Good. But why omit my title?

"Princess Sophia Singh says votes for women!" I scream. The photographers hear my name and in the next second their cameras flash in my face. Suddenly, someone yanks my arm from behind to drag me away from the car. The crowd is being dispersed by the policemen.

"Votes for women!" I shout a final time as the Prime Minister's car drives off.

"Was that really necessary, miss?"

I glance over my shoulder at the man twisting my arm. It is the friendly policeman from before, except he doesn't look so friendly now.

"Let go of my arm!" I snap.

His hold tightens. "You're coming with me."

I am shoved into a police cart and driven to Scotland Yard. As I sit in a chair, waiting to be formally arrested, another policeman approaches me.

"You're free to go."

"I'm not to be arrested for my violent act against the Prime Minister?" I ask incredulously.

"No, Princess," he says, emphasizing my title. "We're not going to give you free publicity by arresting you."

I scowl at him. I am one of the few suffragettes that has yet to see the inside of a prison cell.

The next day, the newspapers do not fail to publish my pictures. Smiling broadly, I pick up the *Sheffield Daily Telegraph* and gaze at the headline – 'Princess As Picket'.

Well, I may have failed to be arrested on this occasion, but I am sure a second opportunity will come soon.

Chapter 18

Letters to Bamba

1911

I miss Bamba and Catherine so much.

Catherine is incredibly pleased with my suffragette activities and has even become a supporter by donating money. I fill my letters to Bamba with details of all that I do, hoping to impress my big sister. I share with her my thrill at breaking the law by spoiling the census paper that every person in the country is required to complete.

Rather than filling out the boxes, I wrote: "NO VOTE. NO CENSUS" and added "AS WOMEN DO NOT COUNT, THEY REFUSE TO BE COUNTED".

I was following Emmeline's clear instructions: "We must disobey and disrupt!"

As I sign my letter to Bamba with love, I wonder if she would recognize the woman I have become. I've always been her baby sister, the shy, quiet one who adored the fanciest clothes from Paris and was happiest with her horses and dogs.

The pampered princess so different from Bamba, who was always the forthright one. My big sister would make such a marvellous suffragette. I am sure that if she'd remained in England, she would have become one of the leaders, just like Emmeline. Her defiant personality would have been wonderful for the cause and all those policemen and politicians wouldn't have known what had hit them. Papa's *sherni* would have roared in their hypocritical faces.

The light outside is fading fast. I am at my desk with pen and paper at hand. I've been sitting here for the last half-hour, trying to find the words to write to Bamba. I don't know where to begin. I am so distraught. I wish Bamba were here to give me a reassuring hug instead of being thousands of miles away. I put the pen down. Perhaps I should try again tomorrow after a good night's rest. But my sleep is restless because of all the horror stories I hear and the guilt I feel. Will I really be in a more powerful state of mind tomorrow? Perhaps I should just empty my mind on to the paper and see if it makes any sense. I can always tear up the letter if it doesn't start again. I pick up the pen, taking a deep breath. I begin to write.

123

Princess Bamba Duleep Singh
Lahore, Punjab
India

Dear Bamba,

I am writing to you now with my heart breaking. My friends have been sent to prison by the government for demanding our rights. The suffragettes insist that they are not criminals and are refusing to eat a single thing. They have gone on hunger strike to protest. The government will not allow them the status of political prisoners and has ordered that the women be force-fed.

I have heard such horrid tales of what these poor women are enduring. A tube is inserted through the nose or mouth into the stomach, and liquid food is then passed down the tube. Emmeline and I were discussing it and she told me that the prisons are a place of horror and torment. Sickening scenes of violence take place almost every hour of the day, as doctors go from cell to cell performing this hideousness. She says that she will never forget the screams of the women who are force-fed.

It is quite barbaric, but I must admire the women who remain true to the cause. Alas, I am denied such opportunities. No matter what I do, no matter how many stones I throw, the police refuse to charge me with a crime.

It is becoming a burden to be Queen Vi's god-daughter. They think that to arrest and imprison me will lead to embarrassment for the King, so I am to be left alone.

Emmeline has assured me that I must not lose heart, and that I am useful to the cause in so many other ways, through my fundraising and publicity work. No matter where I go, the newspaper photographers follow me. I am the princess whose picture must appear in the press for the suffragette cause.

I suppose Emmeline is right. We must all serve the cause in the best way we can. If money and glamour are what I can offer, then I shall offer those things.

The other thing I have to mention is that although the campaign is gathering pace, there are some women who are abandoning the cause.

A few nights ago, several suffragettes from

the militant section used hammers to smash the windows of buildings in central London. A lot of shops were targeted, but no theft occurred because we are not thieves. We are merely making a point, but some suffragettes have quit our movement because they perceive this violence to be unacceptable.

Between you and me, I do not think the women leaving are real suffragettes. How can they claim to be when they run away the moment the campaign moves up a notch?

The most notable deserter is Elizabeth Garrett Anderson. You remember she was your heroine? You wanted to follow in her footsteps and become a doctor, like her. The really sad thing to report is that she has abandoned us at the first sign of trouble.

Emmeline assures us in her confident manner that what we are doing is necessary.

"We are not breaking windows and cutting telegraph wires in order to win the approval of the people who were attacked. If the general public were pleased with what we are doing, that would be proof that our tactics are ineffective. We don't intend the *people to be pleased."*

Emmeline is right. Her words have reinforced our confidence.

Bamba, darling, sometimes in life we have to accept that simply waving placards in Hyde Park is just not going to bring change. A group of women chanting in a park does not really affect men's everyday lives, does it?

This is a revolution and I am so proud to be a part of it. I feel so much better now that I have written this letter and shared my thoughts. Talking with you always helps so much. I still wish you were here with me!

With all my love,

Soph x

A few weeks later, my maid places a letter next to my breakfast tray.

"Eeek!" A gleeful sound escapes me as I notice the Indian postmark.

Grabbing it, I hurry to the garden to sit in my favourite chair under the tree. The maid follows with the tray and arranges it on the small table beside me.

I tear the envelope open.

Princess Sophia Duleep Singh
Faraday House
Hampton Court Palace
England

Dear Soph,

How are you, my darling? I read your last letter with joy. So your sister suffragettes are breaking windows now and cutting telegraph wires. How absolutely wonderful!

I'm not sure if your high-profile supporters will stick around for the long haul. It looks like it's hotting up and 'respectable' people usually desert because they can't stand the heat. They only want to be involved when everything is rosy.

Darling, do be careful. I know you feel guilty about not being treated equally by the police but I suppose it's a blessing. Do you really want to be force-fed in a prison, like some goose being fattened up for a feast?

Now let me tell you about my own adventures. I'm having the loveliest time as the Princess of Punjab.

I went along to a party the other day and wore a traditional outfit in the latest design, where you just wear a short blouse and a skirt with the midriff

showing. It was a lovely green colour and I thought
I resembled a peacock in beauty and majesty. But
you should have seen the expressions on some of the
English women! Honestly, they would have curdled
milk. The women were scandalized at seeing a bare
waist. I find it very strange that they should behave
in this way. They're not scandalized when the Indian
women wear their traditional clothes. So why me?
Why should I wear a corset and high-collar dress just
because I was born and raised in England? The heat
is unbearable here and it is no wonder so many
Englishwomen are always fainting.

Anyway, stop trying to lure me back to England.
I shall never return.

Oh, and as the suffragettes mean so much to you,
here's another donation.

Smash those windows!

Lots of love,

Bamba

Chapter 19

Pillar Boxes

1912

My sister-in-law Anne and I are enjoying the loveliest walk in Richmond. I've chosen this route for our exercise as I must post my letters to Bamba and Catherine directly inside the post office.

As we walk arm-in-arm, Anne has not an inkling as to why we have come so far for our exercise. Instead, I take the opportunity to confide my feelings of insecurity to her.

"I don't think I will ever be like Bamba," I say.

Anne gives me an odd sideways look. She loves Bamba like family, but I know she finds my big sister a little intimidating. "Why would you want to?"

"So that I may be able to express how I feel," I say. "I flush a beetroot colour when I have an audience of more than five before me. I'm still no different to the shy little girl that I was."

Anne nods sympathetically. "Why do you want to change now?"

"Emmeline has asked me to speak at a rally," I say with none of the excitement I should rightfully feel. Anne continues to nod, encouraging me to go on.

"I have of course refused. How can I do it? I have none of her confidence or Bamba's. I wish I did. I so wish I could rouse the crowds like Emmeline and her daughters, Christabel and Sylvia. Their passion is marked in every word about our right to vote. I thought about taking public speaking lessons but frankly, I don't think they would help. The butterflies in my stomach, combined with my dry mouth, will leave me looking a fool on any platform."

Anne takes her time to find the words. Finally, when we've walked a few metres in silence, she says, "But you are happiest in the background, organizing and supporting. That is your strength."

I absorb Anne's advice. Actually, she does have a point. I do not have the gift to pull people out of their slumber and to call them to revolution. And that is perfectly fine. I should focus on my own struggles and—

"Good afternoon, Princess Sophia."

I stiffen. I know who the voice belongs to and I turn slowly to face the sergeant of the Richmond police station. Adopting my most regal pose, I nod in acknowledgement at the tall, burly man towering over me.

He doffs his policeman's helmet to me and Anne. "What brings you here to the post office?"

"Why does anyone come to the post office?" I reply mildly.

"You tell me," he says.

Anne gives him a look as if he is quite mad. "To post her letters, of course."

"Servants on holiday, are they?" His tone is mocking.

Anne suddenly looks lost for words. She questions me with her eyes to say, "Yes, why are you posting the letters yourself?"

I flash my brightest smile. "I prefer to do some things myself, especially when I am out on a walk with my dogs. My sisters are abroad in India and Germany, and I like to inform them about events in England."

He frowns slightly. "We are investigating a very serious matter here."

"Oh?" I raise wide, innocent eyes at him. "What happened?"

"You expect me to believe that you don't know?" he demands.

"Sergeant, I don't play games," I shoot back.

Anne is now looking appalled at the sergeant's behaviour. "Now look here, officer—"

He cuts her off by raising a hand and then removes the helmet from his head. "Ma'am, a very serious crime has been committed."

He succeeds in subduing Anne. I, on the other hand, refuse to be intimidated. In a pompous voice I say, "I'm all ears, Sergeant."

"Somebody poured ink and tar inside the pillar boxes in Richmond," he declares. "The letters inside have all been ruined. That is a crime. It is illegal to tamper with the property of the Royal Mail."

I must play my part and clap a hand over my mouth. "Heavens!"

"And do you know what was pasted on to these pillar boxes?" He watches me closely, as if he expects me to squirm. I hold my ground.

"I have no idea."

"Leaflets that had 'Votes for Women' printed on them," he states.

"Goodness me!" I exclaim.

"Oh dear," Anne mumbles and takes a step back. I can tell she no longer wants to be a part of this conversation. Or rather interrogation.

"So, Princess Sophia," the sergeant coughs dryly. "I must ask you this question."

"Please do."

"As a member of the WSPU, can you tell me anything about this crime?"

"I cannot."

"Indeed, let me rephrase the question," he says. "Were you a participant in this vandalism?"

"Sergeant! Really!" I object, placing a hand on my heart. "I'm offended you would accuse me of such a thing."

"Offended are you now, Princess?"

"Yes, actually I am," I declare. "I mean, do you have any evidence against me?"

"I think the leaflets are my evidence," he says. "It's a calling card."

"But you can't trace it to me," I point out. "There are thousands of suffragettes. What are you going to do? Arrest us all?"

His eyes narrow. "You would like that, wouldn't you?"

"To be arrested?" I ask. "Oh, you have no idea how hard I have tried."

"Indeed, you have."

"So why won't you arrest me?" I demand.

"Princess." He spits the title out. "Our orders are from the top. The princess is not to be touched. It's a real privilege to be the god-daughter of a queen."

"A dead queen."

"But still a queen."

I am irritated now. "If I claim responsibility, will you arrest me?"

"No, I will not arrest you, but I will arrest all the members of your local branch."

I cannot allow that to happen.

"Well, will you look at the time?" I say, turning away and grabbing Anne's hand. "Must dash."

We hurry across the road to push open the post-office door.

"Good afternoon, Princess Sophia." The clerk is not surprised to see me as I have visited twice already.

"I am in a hurry today," I say, passing him the letters and coins for payment. Anne stands beside me, constantly looking over her shoulder.

"Of course." The clerk produces three stamps and proceeds to lick them before pasting them on to my lovely, pastel-coloured envelopes.

The task completed, Anne and I walk out on to the street. She looks relieved that the sergeant is nowhere in sight.

"Soph," she says. "I don't think you should worry so much about being shy."

I glance at her, confused. "How do you mean?"

"Well, you were anything but shy with that policeman," she says. "You might not be able to stand on stage in front of hundreds of people, but I think you are quite capable of standing up for yourself."

"Thank you, Anne," I say. "That means a lot."

She looks directly into my eyes. "Now tell me, have you been damaging pillar boxes?"

I give her my most sincere look. "No, I haven't been directly involved, but it seems to be creating a reaction with the general public. People are outraged at having their letters destroyed."

"You would be annoyed too, wouldn't you?"

I allow myself a small smile. "Why else would I come all the way to the Richmond post office?"

Chapter 20

A Salesgirl

1912

"Come and get it!" I shout. "*The Suffragette!*"

I am standing outside the gates of Hampton Court Palace with my sandwich board, selling our newspaper, *The Suffragette*.

"Votes for women!"

"What's this?" An elderly lady stops to peer at the front page of my newspaper. I have never seen her before.

I adjust the strap of my bag across my shoulder and beam at her. "This is the suffragette paper, which has all the news about our campaign to win the vote for women. Do buy one."

"Well, why not?" she says. "There is a lot of coverage in the main newspapers. Let me read what you all have to say about it."

She hands over the money. "Thank you, dear. If it is intriguing enough, I shall come back again."

"Please do that!" I say warmly.

My next customer is not so friendly. It is a resident of Hampton Court Palace who is a general's widow. For the life of me I cannot remember her name.

"Sophia Singh," she snaps.

She has not used my title and it is not a greeting. It is a statement. I am aware of the increased hostility from my neighbours since I joined the suffragettes. They do not approve. They think we are a bunch of troublemakers.

"Good afternoon," I say as pleasantly as I can manage. Catherine has advised me not to take the bait and to remain calm when I am confronted.

"Is it true?" she demands.

"I am not a mind reader," I reply sweetly. "Is what true?"

"That we are to expect a raid here by the police?"

"Why?"

"The newspaper is saying that you troublemakers rioted again and smashed windows near Parliament a few days ago. The police raided your headquarters to arrest one of your ringleaders, Christabel Pankhurst, but she escaped."

"Oh."

"And that you helped her escape. Sophia, you must

tell me the truth. Is that preposterous Pankhurst woman hiding in Faraday House?"

I take a deep breath to control my irritation. "No, she isn't, and I did not help her get away."

"Then why are the papers saying you did?"

"The papers write all sorts of rubbish to make the news exciting, and—" I fix her with a direct stare, "—nothing sells newspapers more than when princesses are mentioned."

She bites her lip. I can guess that she wants to retort something about my family being dispossessed from our kingdom. These types of snide remarks have been directed at me and my sisters our entire lives. It usually comes from English women who want to bring us down a peg or two. Bamba used to get the brunt of it. They hated her for refusing to believe they were superior to us because of their skin colour. How I wish Bamba were here to put this jumped-up nobody in her place. She is only living here because her husband got himself killed in India.

Sometimes it does cross my mind that we are also fighting for the rights of women like this. Women who are too dim to see that they stand to benefit if we win. But no, they would prefer to pander to men's sensibilities.

"I have no time for this," I snap, wishing I could

remember her name. "Either purchase a paper, or kindly go on your way."

Her mouth falls open in outrage, but I maintain my steely gaze. Muttering under her breath, she turns to stomp away.

I do not know why the newspapers are lying about me. I was nowhere near headquarters that night and Christabel escaped without my help.

"Well, well, well, Princess Sophia the salesgirl."

"Anne!" I turn at the sound of her voice and throw my arms around her neck. "What are you doing here?"

"Victor's busy in London with some business so I thought I'd come to visit you."

"Oh, I'm so glad," I say. "Come and stand to my left. The passersby need to be able to see the stand."

"Oh." Anne eyes the stack of newspapers. "Are we going to sell all of them?"

"Just a few more and then we'll go inside for some tea and scones."

She nods and then visibly jumps when I call out, "*The Suffragette*!"

"Soph!"

"Sorry," I say sheepishly. "I have to call for attention in order to sell them."

Anne takes a step back and I guess that she doesn't want me yelling in her ear. It is when she pulls her fur closer around her neck that I decide to pack up for the day. My sister-in-law has come to visit and I should be more hospitable. I look over the road to my footman. He helped set up my stall and is on hand in case I need him. I wave a hand and he hurries over.

"I'm done for today," I instruct him. "Please pack up."

He immediately sets to work and I link my arm with Anne's.

"Don't let me stop you from selling them," she says.

"I'll come back tomorrow," I reassure her. "Now tell me what you've been up to."

Anne shrugs her dainty shoulders and I admire her new fur. It has been a while since I've placed an order for new clothes at the dressmakers. I just haven't had the time or interest, to be honest.

"Victor and I are just sailing along," she says. "But I'm more interested in you. It's all hotting up now, isn't it? Victor was very concerned to read a newspaper article about you at the Bow Street Magistrates' Court."

"Oh yes," I enthuse. "I was there hand-in-hand with my friend Muriel, the Countess de la Warr. We were jostled by the crowd, but the policemen allowed us to pass inside once we were searched."

Anne looks appalled. "Good grief! You were searched?"

I nod. "We weren't allowed to take in any items like food, books or pamphlets. No banners. Nothing."

"Why?" Anne looks perplexed.

I giggle. "Because in the past, suffragettes have thrown rotten tomatoes at the prosecutors below."

"But why were you there in the first place?"

"I was there to support my friends." I admit. "A group of nine suffragettes had been charged with planning arson attacks. The only thing is, no bombs went off. How can they be on trial for events that did not happen? In my eyes, they are innocent, and I was there to support them."

"What happened to them?"

"They were found guilty."

We are in Faraday House now and my dogs come running to greet us. Anne pets one of them and then turns to me with worried eyes. "Soph, Victor and I can't help being concerned about your involvement in all this. What started out as waving placards in Hyde Park is becoming quite dangerous."

"You mustn't worry," I say dismissively, flopping down on the sofa. "I know I will be on the right side of history."

Chapter 21

The King's Horse

1913

The Epsom Derby is today.

I have one of the best seats in the grounds, even though I am not in the royal box. Unlike Queen Vi and Uncle Bertie, King George V and his wife, Queen Mary, do not really concern themselves with me.

Well, actually that is not quite true.

I hear from the gossipmongers at Hampton Court Palace that my activities have been brought to King George's attention. He, of course, does not approve of my suffragette campaigning and views me with embarrassment. I have even heard that he would like to see me removed from my home at Faraday House. Quite an outrageous thing to suggest really, seeing as it was his own grandmother Queen Vi, my godmother, who gifted me the house. And anyway, I do not live there for free. I have never missed a single rent payment.

The King has his own horse in the race. He is a fine stallion called Anmer, but out of all the fifteen horses running today, my money is on the favourite, Craganour.

I smile at the man standing beside me. It is so wonderful to be spending time with my brother. I haven't seen Freddie for ages and when he invited me to join him at the races, I agreed right away. Victor and Anne have now moved to Paris and Freddie is the only family I have left in England.

"Bets on, Soph?" Freddie asks.

"Of course." I wave my betting slip.

"There must be about half a million spectators," Freddie says, casting an eye on the crowd all around us and below. "Epsom's always a good turnout."

"I'm so pleased you invited me," I say.

"Well, I hardly ever see you these days," Freddie grumbles. "You're so busy with all your lady friends."

"Suffragettes," I correct him. "That's what we're called."

He frowns slightly. "You know, one reads all sorts of things in the papers. Women going to jail where they are force-fed and hurt. Grim stuff."

I nod. "It's just awful how they treat women."

"I worry about you, Soph. I don't want you to go to prison."

I roll my eyes. "No chance of that, dear brother. Being a god-daughter to Queen Vi prevents that."

"You're a very lucky girl then," Freddie says gravely. "You are protected."

"I don't want to be protected," I snap, annoyed that he does not understand how much I feel left out of my own cause because of my privilege.

"Those women who go to prison are tough," Freddie says, pushing his fingers through his hair. "Are you sure you would be able to withstand what they do to prisoners?"

I raise my chin in defiance. "I am tough! I've just never been given the opportunity to prove myself."

Freddie shakes his head. "Let's not argue today, Soph. I've missed seeing you and you're the only sister that still lives in England. I haven't seen Bamba in a long time and Catherine hardly ever visits from Germany."

"You could always visit them," I suggest. "They would love to entertain their brother in their new countries."

Freddie pretends to shudder. "No thank you. I am an Englishman, and an Englishman does not leave his castle."

I laugh and poke his arm.

"The race is about to begin," Freddie cries. Sure enough, the starting gun sounds and the horses are off. "Come on, Craganour!"

"Come on!" I cheer. "Craganour! Go!"

Suddenly I see movement down on the track. Some of the horses have sped past already, but a few are still catching up. There is a woman in the path of these horses. My hand flies to my mouth. It is a woman in suffragette white. I peer at the figure through my binoculars, but I cannot make out who she is.

"Freddie! Look!" I cry.

"I see her! A madwoman!"

"She'll be trampled!"

It is too late. A horse gallops around the corner and collides with the woman. She somersaults through the air and lands on the ground like a broken doll. The jockey is thrown off the horse and is lying a few feet away.

"It's the King's horse!" Freddie shouts above the uproar of the crowd. "That's Anmer on the ground. The jockey's down, too!

"Oh…" I can barely speak and I cling to the lapel of Freddie's jacket. A crowd of officials move forward to surround the woman and she disappears from view.

My last glimpse is of her lying completely still.

Is she dead?

Today is the funeral of the suffragette.

Our first martyr.

Her name was Emily Wilding Davison, and she gave her life for women's right to vote. Emily never regained consciousness after her collision with the horse and died four days later. They say her skull was fractured. I did not recognize her in those few seconds when she ran out into the path of the King's horse. I had met Emily a number of times in the company of Emmeline. She was tall and slender, with a head of red hair.

Nearly five thousand people come out to watch her funeral procession from the church to King's Cross Station. We suffragettes form a guard of honour around the coffin. After the church service, her body is to be transferred to Northumberland. She will be buried in her home town of Morpeth.

I am sitting on the train, part of the group that is accompanying Emily's coffin home. We are wearing our white dresses, but with black sashes to mark the mourning of our comrade, our sister, our soldier.

Ada Wright is beside me. She was present on Black

Friday and it was her picture that the *Daily Mirror* newspaper plastered all over its front page the next day. It was an image that truly shocked people as Ada lay semi-conscious on the ground after a policeman had battered her. We didn't know each other then, but have become firm friends since.

"Do you think Emily wanted to commit suicide?" A young woman I do not know asks aloud.

"No!" I snap. "Why would she?"

"For the suffragette cause."

I shake my head. "I don't think Emily had planned to end her life. I heard that she had a return train ticket in her pocket, and she was planning to speak at a suffragette meeting the following day."

"Then how did she end up under the horse's hooves?" Another voice pipes up.

"I think she miscalculated," I say. "Many of the horses had already passed her when she ducked under the railing to run out. I think she was only intending to unfurl the two suffragette banners so everybody at the racecourse would see."

"What banners?"

"The ones hidden inside her coat."

"You seem very sure."

"Epsom is laid out like a horseshoe," I explain. "She was positioned where the racecourse bends. I do think this was a terrible accident. Emily had so much more to do, so much fight in her. I don't think she would choose suicide."

Ada is silent throughout this discussion. I can't help wondering if she is thinking of her near brush with death on Black Friday.

For the rest of the journey, we remember Emily with stories. The most infamous one is when she firebombed a house in Surrey which belonged to the Chancellor of the Exchequer, David Lloyd George. The house was empty at the time and no lives were lost. In our struggle, it is Emily's life that has been lost.

We reach Morpeth to find the streets packed with crowds. Some are saying that almost twenty thousand people have lined up to pay their respects to one of their own.

I stand amongst the people to watch Emily's coffin as it is lowered into the ground. Her name will be added to the martyrs' list, under the women who lost their lives days after suffering injuries on Black Friday.

History remembers the martyrs of every cause and I do believe that Emily's name will be known to all in the years to come. Every girl in the country will know her, be it now, in fifty years or even one hundred years from today.

To sacrifice your life is noble.

And history remembers the noble.

Chapter 22

In Court At Last

1913

"Don't worry," my lawyer whispers in my ear. "They won't lock you up for this."

It is not for want of trying!

I say nothing as I stand beside him at Feltham Court to answer for my non-payment of taxes. According to the law, I am obliged to pay for a licence to keep two dogs, a carriage and a groomsman. I have made no payment and obtained no licences.

Why would I pay when I have helped to set up the Women's Tax Resistance League? Through my own donations and much fundraising, we have produced pamphlets to advise our two hundred members to stop paying taxes.

I pull my black fur tightly around my shoulders, but

make sure that my badge and medal of the Tax Resistance League are visible. I glance back at my friends, the six suffragettes who have come along to support me. Amongst them are Ada and Gertrude Eaton, who I get on with really well.

Gertrude is the secretary of the Women's Tax Resistance League. She is the one who gave me tuition on how to control the butterflies in my stomach and project my voice so that people could hear me. I knew this day was coming and I have prepared my speech in advance. I so wish I could speak publicly without notes like Emmeline. Unfortunately, I am not blessed with her confidence or my sister Bamba's and so I must rely on handwritten notes.

I try to calm myself. My voice needs to sound assured and I am anxious that if it trembles with nerves, I will let the side down.

My lawyer clears his throat. "My client would like to say a few words in her defence, if the court would permit it."

The magistrate frowns. He is an old man, probably bald under that wig he is wearing. It seems to me that he would rather be anywhere but here listening to reports of the illegal activities of upper-class women.

"You may proceed," he mutters.

I straighten my back and lift my chin. Una had told me that we must always project our voices. Here goes. I begin to read.

"I am unable to pay money to the state, as I am not allowed to have any say in the way in which it is spent. Neither am I allowed a voice in the choosing of Members of Parliament, whose salaries I have to help pay. This is very unjustified. When the women of England are given the vote and the State acknowledges me as a citizen, I shall, of course, pay my share willingly towards its upkeep." I pause to take a deep breath before I deliver my final rehearsed line. "If I am not a fit person for the purposes of representation, why should I be a fit person for taxation?"

A round of applause breaks out behind me from my friends. I turn and grin at them.

The judge glares at us angrily. "Order!"

A hush falls in the room again. It is clear that the magistrate is not impressed by any of it, but we do not care. We are here to make a point.

The magistrate clears his throat. "The defendant's political views are of no interest to this court. She is guilty of not obeying the law. She is hereby fined twelve pounds and ten shillings for failure to pay for the required licences."

Taking a deep breath, I launch into the words I already prepared in my mind before setting foot in this court. "I will not be paying the fine, sir."

There is a small gasp in the courtroom. It has not come from the suffragettes, for they expected this from me. It is the men, the practitioners of the law, who are astounded at my defiance.

The magistrate seems to be at the end of his tether. "Then the bailiff shall pay you a visit!"

I walk away with a spring in my step. At last! An acknowledgement of my law-breaking. The Crown may have ordered that I may not be thrown into prison for the embarrassment it would cause the king, but it cannot stop a court from recording that I have broken a law.

The magistrate remains true to his word and the bailiffs come to my door. Without so much as a how-do-you-do, they storm into my house when my maid opens the front door. She squeals when they push her aside.

I run after them. Una had warned me that bailiffs always head for a lady's bedroom where her jewellery is usually stored.

"Don't you dare lay a finger on my property!" I scream. "Don't you dare!"

They of course ignore me as they have been trained to do. One even pushes me aside as I try to yank his arm. I watch helplessly as they attack my furniture. Drawers are opened and flung on the floor as the men search for valuables, and even some of my exquisite Parisian gowns are strewn on the bed.

How absolutely dare they! I knew this was going to happen but to be actually faced with burly, mean-looking men touching my things is unsettling. I am furious.

"This will do!" One of them holds up my pearl choker. He raises it to his teeth and licks one of the 131 pearls. I want to throttle him. "It's real. Anything else?"

His accomplice holds up my gold bracelet, which is studded with diamonds. "Very sparkly," he comments.

And then they leave as quickly as they entered my home.

I make my way to the hallway. My maid is still standing by the door, sobbing.

"Did they hurt you, Princess?" she cries.

I place an arm around her. "No, they didn't. They were bailiffs, just here to snatch what they can to cover a debt. Are you all right? You're still shaking."

"That big one could have broken me into two pieces," she says dramatically. "I could have snapped in half, he pushed me so hard."

I pat her back. "There, there. You'll be fine. Take the day off if you need to."

We find out that my jewellery will be up for auction at Twickenham Town Hall in March. My friends and I pack out the hall. We are wearing our white gowns with purple sashes, visibly identifiable as suffragettes. The auctioneer scowls at me as I take my seat in the front row. He has probably been warned that I would turn up. Either he recognizes me from the pictures the *Daily Mail* keep printing of me, or he just searched the crowd for the brown-skinned suffragette.

I have come prepared with a speech again. But this time, I have spent hours rehearsing it in front of the mirror. I am determined to speak to the room as a natural public speaker rather than one that must always read from a piece of paper.

Just when the auctioneer looks set to begin with the clearing of his throat, I rise to my feet and present my back to him. I face the hall and speak loudly and clearly: "I protest against this sale, seeing it is most unjust to women that they should be compelled to pay taxes, when they have no voice in the government of the country."

The room bursts into applause. Glad that my bit is

done, I retake my seat, urging the trembling of my hands to stop. Goodness, I do hate public speaking, but I am glad to say that I was able to speak today because of the tips I was given.

I throw a quick glance at my close friends, Gertrude and Ada, who are here to support me. Gertrude is bidding on my jewellery. There is only one other bidder.

The auctioneer's hammer bangs down. The sale is complete. Gertrude has won the lot for a fraction of the value of my jewellery. She pays ten pounds for the pearls and seven pounds for the bracelet. When it's all over, Ada runs up to me outside and gives me a big hug. "You were wonderful and spoke so well."

I blush a little at the compliment. Gertrude catches up to us and hands me a velvet pouch. "I believe this is yours."

I smile at her. "Thank you, my friend."

She smiles back. "Deeds not words."

Chapter 23

Cat and Mouse

1914

I am on my way to a house in Campden Hill Square in Kensington, known to us suffragettes as 'Mouse Castle'. It is the safe haven for those hiding from the police and is owned by a suffragette.

Emmeline intends to send a message to the government tonight.

She has been in prison, sentenced to three years for the arson attack on the house of the Chancellor of the Exchequer. It was actually the work of Emily Davison, our friend who was killed on the racecourse. The house had been empty and no one was hurt, but the police charged Emmeline with incitement. That means she encouraged others to do it. She could not very well deny that she incited the act, as she is always saying in her public speeches that we need to break the law. Deeds not words.

Like all the other suffragettes in prison, Emmeline began a hunger strike and the authorities had to release her. She had weakened so much that they were afraid she would die. Under no circumstances does the government want Emmeline's death on their hands. It would make her a martyr and the officials have no doubt that there would be riots in the streets of Britain.

Emmeline was released under the 'Cat and Mouse Act' which means that she was transferred out of prison to a house, in order to get better. There, she received medical attention and was guarded round the clock by a policeman. Suffragettes who are released under this law must not meet other suffragettes or speak publicly. It is what I think they call house arrest. Once a suffragette has recovered, she must return to prison to complete her sentence.

As if Emmeline had any intention to do so!

I am aware that Emmeline escaped the house two nights ago. The policeman who was meant to be guarding her has probably now been sacked. Emmeline is taunting the police. She placed an advert in a newspaper yesterday, informing the readers that she intends to speak publicly in Campden Hill Square tonight. She intends to rally the troops once again in the cause for votes for women.

My friend Ada and I reach the square just after seven in the evening. I thought we would be the first to arrive, but we are not. It is already packed with nearly a thousand people: some suffragettes, as well as others who are against us. Also visible are the police officers with their truncheons. We know what we must do. The instruction was passed on to us last night in secret. We are ready.

"Are you nervous?" Ada asks in a low voice.

I give her a bright smile. "No. It will go according to plan."

An hour later, at eight o'clock precisely, Emmeline steps out on to the balcony of the house at Number Two. I can tell it is her, even though she is wearing a black veil over her face, much like the *niqab* that I saw some royal Muslim women wear on my trip to India.

A hush falls on the crowd as more and more people notice the figure high up above us. For a moment, I think of the scene before me as a miniature version of the Buckingham Palace balcony. Queen Vi used to appear there on occasions to wave down at her subjects in the mall.

Emmeline is a queen tonight.

Our queen leading us to victory soon.

I think of the English queen, Boudicca. Is this how her followers viewed her as she led them into battle?

Or Queen Elizabeth as she inspired her people to fight and defeat the invading Spanish Armada?

It is a cold February night, but it is not the chilly air that is causing the shivers to race down my spine. It is the anticipation of what will happen here tonight.

Suddenly there is a collective gasp as Emmeline lifts her veil to reveal her face.

A pin-drop silence and then she speaks. "They know little what women are. Women are very slow to rouse, but once they are aroused, once they are determined, nothing on earth and nothing in heaven will make women give way. It is impossible. And so this Cat and Mouse Act which is being used against women today has failed. They have to choose between giving us freedom or giving us death!"

Half the crowd breaks into applause and the other half jeers.

Emmeline raises her hand and the crowd quietens. "I have reached London tonight in spite of armies of police. I am here tonight and not a man is going to protect me, because this is a women's fight, and we are going to protect ourselves! I am coming out amongst you in a few minutes and I challenge the government to rearrest me."

The police officers in the square do not wait to hear any more. They collectively surge towards the house just as Emmeline steps back off the balcony.

I am ready.

Before the police can storm the house, the first guard of suffragettes steps out of the front door. People around me will not be able to see, but I know that they are surrounding the woman in black, and that she will be wearing her face veil again. It is part of the plan. The suffragettes' arms are linked. They step out into the square, defiant and daring anyone to break the chain apart.

The crowd sways inwards but the guard is strong. I exchange a look with Ada. We are in position as we were instructed. I count in my head: *five, four, three, two* and Ada and I step in to become the outer circle for the veiled figure. Our plan is to get out of the square. It is not easy. I am jostled and pushed but I hold my ground. My arms are linked with Ada on one side and another suffragette on the other. There is a shout in the crowd. "We cannot allow Mrs Pankhurst to be arrested!"

And that is it. The police have had enough. They have already been embarrassed by Emmeline's escape from house arrest. They have no intention of letting her make a fool of them again.

"Charge!"

The policemen barge us with their truncheons. But this is no Black Friday. We suffragettes did not come unprepared this time.

A number of women pull out their own weapons in the form of hard, solid rolling pins. And the fight begins. Policemen hit women with their truncheons and the suffragettes beat them back. My task is to maintain the circle, so I have come unarmed. In reality, we cannot out-bludgeon the policemen. They are men. They are bigger and stronger, and the suffragettes are soon falling to the ground, bloodied and bruised.

I am one of them. Although I try to remain on my feet, I am pushed down by the sheer force around me. My face hits the ground and I feel a numbness and then an almighty pain. It is as if my head is on fire. I press my forehead to ease the burning and manage to look up. The tumble of the outer circle has meant that the inner guard has fallen too. The police are only feet away from the veiled figure. From this odd angle, I see a truncheon lift in the air before it comes crashing down on her head. She collapses to the ground. I stare at her limp body and can only assume she is unconscious.

The plan is working, I think as several policemen lift the figure and carry her away as if she is laid out in a coffin.

Despite the pain in my head, I manage a secret smile. They will realize when they are at the police station that the veiled woman is not Emmeline at all. It is our decoy, Florence Smith, who shares Emmeline's physical build.

Hah! Emmeline has escaped. Our plan has worked. The police have been fooled again.

"OW!"

My thoughts are interrupted as I am manhandled by a police officer. He hauls me to my feet and arrests me. I grin at Ada. She too is looking overjoyed that the plan worked.

As usual, I am released without charge.

Ada, on the other hand, is sentenced to fourteen days in jail. I cannot bear it and am filled with guilt that my friend will have to suffer prison whilst I am free. I decide to pay Ada's fine and she is released.

Ada does not thank me for my generosity.

"Why did you do that?" she demands, marching up to me in the grounds of Hampton Court Palace as I walk my dogs. "Why did you pay the fine? We suffragettes are making a point when we go to prison."

I gaze at her helplessly. "I just had to!" I blurt. "It wasn't fair that you were sent to prison and I was not. I'm sorry."

My apology appeases Ada somewhat. "I don't understand. You have broken the law so many times.

Why won't they send you to prison? Even Mrs Pankhurst has been to prison."

"It's because of my association with the royal family," I explain, a little embarrassed. "I am a god-daughter of Queen Victoria and it would embarrass King George if I were hauled off to prison."

"Would it really?" Ada doesn't look convinced.

"I have thrown myself at the Prime Minister's car," I say. "I have refused to pay my taxes; I was present outside Parliament on Black Friday and yet none of it was enough to send me to prison. The orders have come directly from the top."

"Oh well, I'm not sure that's such a bad thing," Ada says. "You could do a lot worse in terms of damage and get away with it."

"It pains me greatly that I am left out of the struggle," I say sadly. "All these women are making huge sacrifices by going to prison and I am denied that."

Ada links her arm through mine. "Come on, Soph, you can contribute in other ways. The photographers love you. We have made the papers so many times because you have been with us in our cause. You've given us so much free publicity."

I look at her doubtfully. "You think so?"

Ada nods. "Glamour. That is what you give us. Glamour."

We both burst out laughing.

"You have a status that links you to the royal family and you also have money. Give those two things to our cause."

I nod. Ada's right. I shall increase my donations to the WSPU.

That very day, I donate £51.00 out of my annual income of £600.

Chapter 24

War

1914

My carriage rocks a little and I clutch the safety bar as it speeds along the route to a meeting with Emmeline and the suffragettes. A gathering has been called urgently in response to the announcement of war.

The British Empire is now at war with Imperial Germany. It all started in the strangest way. A Serb nationalist, I think, murdered the Archduke of Austria and his wife, and suddenly we are fighting the Germans and a few other countries too. The prime minister, Mr Asquith, has declared that we can no longer continue with 'business as usual' and that the country must come together to defeat the enemy. The men must sign up either to the navy or the army, and we women who are left behind must do our bit to help run the country. Some people are quite excited about this war, especially young men, but ever since it was announced, all I can think about is how to get Catherine out of Germany.

It is an awful thought that my sister is behind enemy lines and I haven't been able to sleep because of the worry. I've been writing letters to whoever I think might be able to help, and it's why I am running so late now.

My carriage pulls up outside the elegant house in Kensington and I hurry to the meeting. The room I enter is already full and Emmeline is standing at one end. She catches my eye and gives a slight nod. Gathering my skirt, I sit down on the nearest chair.

"As I was saying, war has broken out and I believe that we should put a halt to our campaign."

There is a murmur of disagreement in the room.

Emmeline raises a hand. "Please listen to me. Our country is at war. We must support the war effort. We are needed as citizens of this country. We must contribute to defending our country. Do you really think we will have a campaign if our country is conquered by the enemy?"

The suffragettes in the room are divided. Some agree with Emmeline. Others do not. I am with our leader.

"The men will be off fighting," Emmeline says. "This is

an opportunity for us to prove ourselves. We can hold the fort and show that we are worthy of the vote."

There is silence in the room as her words are absorbed.

"I have an agreement with the Prime Minister that he will grant us the vote once we win the war."

"But…"

"Don't trust him…"

"He will betray us…"

Emmeline raises her hand again for silence but there are a group of women who are now on their feet.

"We don't agree," one says. "We have sacrificed too much to get where we are. We can't give up now. We refuse to give up."

"Then you cannot be a part of the WSPU," Emmeline snaps. "The Prime Minister has agreed to release all the suffragettes from prison as long as there is no more violence. I have given Asquith my word."

The objectors gawk at Emmeline. Then one says, "Then indeed, we cannot be a part of the WSPU."

They turn to leave, and nobody stops them. As their skirts swish towards the door, my gaze remains on Kitty Marion, who is known to have suffered 232 force-feedings in prison. I can understand her reluctance to give up the cause just because the men have decided to go off to war.

But I side with Emmeline. She has led us here so far and I will be with her until the end. She is right. We must win the war first.

Catherine has managed to get herself out of Germany and is now in Switzerland. That is one less thing to worry about, although I must confess that my mind is occupied with fury.

I am incandescent at the order given by the Viceroy of India, Sir Charles Hardinge.

He commanded thousands of Indian soldiers to fight for Britain, and so the Indian army arrived in Europe to do its duty, to defend Britain and its empire. The fighting has been fierce and there are many casualties. Thousands of wounded soldiers are being brought back from the European mainland to be treated in England. The horrible truth is that the awful Viceroy has ordered that wounded Indian soldiers are not to be treated by nurses as the English soldiers are. Instead, white men, orderlies, will do the nursing even though they aren't trained in medical care. It really is scandalous.

What is it with English men who are appointed viceroys of India? It seems their dislike of brown Indian people is far more intense than that of ordinary English people.

None of my English friends would ever approve of such nonsense. These Indian men have come all this way to fight for King and Country. Their bodies have been torn and bruised by the battles. Why shouldn't they receive proper nursing care? It is for this reason that I have put on the Red Cross uniform. I shall nurse as many as I can myself.

My medical training by the Red Cross is brief. We just don't have the luxury of time because the wounded men arrive in droves from battles that have killed their friends.

I quickly learn how to remove pus from wounds, how to apply a poultice to draw out infection and how to dress wounds. At times I think I am in possession of enough rolls of bandages to create an Egyptian mummy!

Nursing, it seems to me, is about making a patient as comfortable as possible while their body heals from trauma. I am informed that I shall have to make beds, disinfect wards and even feed men with my own hands if they cannot do it for themselves so due to injury.

I absorb the training like a sponge.

My country is at war and I shall do my duty.

Chapter 25

A Nurse

1914–15

The Indian soldier gazes up at me. The bruising around his eyes has reduced but his arm is still in a sling. In terms of injury, he is one of the fortunate ones at the Lady Hardinge Hospital. I have witnessed other men howl in terror, shouting that the shells are falling like rain. I am not sure what it is exactly that these men have experienced, but the trauma has invaded not just their bodies, but their souls.

The soldier lying in the bed studies me with interest. "You look like us, but you don't speak any of our languages?"

I smile at him. "I don't speak Punjabi or Urdu at all well, I'm afraid. I was never taught it."

"You were born here?"

I nod.

"What is your name?"

"Sophia." I leave out my title. I am just a Red Cross nurse here. This is a place of injured and dying men who have fought for our country. Men who have come here all the way from India to fight in a war for King-Emperor and Mother Country. They deserve care and healing.

"What is your name?" I ask.

"Amit."

"How did you join the war?"

He looks at me like I am daft. As if he cannot believe I don't know the answer. "Lord Kitchener ordered it. We are soldiers of the Empire and the Empire called."

"That's the reason?" I find it hard to believe. "Because Lord Kitchener commanded it?"

He chuckles. "Why do young men sign up for war?"

"I don't know. I'm asking you."

"Adventure."

Ah, adventure. That makes more sense.

"Travel and new places to see."

"So, what did you get to see?"

"We set off from India full of excitement and reached Marseilles, France on a cold October day. The weather was not what we expected. We had to march all the way to the Western Front."

"Did you regret coming?" I ask.

He looks at me as if he cannot believe I have asked the question. Finally, he says, "No. We are soldiers. Our duty is to defend and fight. Besides, our commander's words helped morale."

"What were they?"

"In my suitcase under the bed there is a brown leather notebook. Would you please get it for me?"

I oblige and hold out the small notebook. Amit shakes his head. "It is my friend Adil's notebook. He carried it in his pocket all the time. His father was the village postmaster and he taught Adil and a few of us other boys to read and write English. Adil wrote down the words of the commander in his notebook. If you turn to the folded page you can read the commander's speech."

I turn to the page and begin to read the neat handwriting.

"Could you please read it aloud?" Amit asks.

"Of course," I say and clear my throat. "It is written:

"You are the descendants of the men who have been mighty rulers and great warriors for many centuries. You will never forget this. You will recall the glories of your race. Hindu and Muslim will be fighting side by side with British soldiers and our gallant French allies. You will be helping to make history. You will be the first Indian soldiers of the King-Emperor, who will have the honour of showing Europe that the sons of India have lost none of their martial instincts."

I close the notebook. I do not ask why Amit has a notebook that belongs to another man. I know the answer. Instead, I simply say, "Quite a speech."

He nods. "It was. It inspired us. There is nothing like flattery and history combined to make men feel invincible."

"You marched to Flanders?"

"We were part of the defence at Wipers."

"Wipers?" I repeat. Where on earth was that?

Amit chuckles. "It is spelled 'Ypres', but we soldiers all pronounced it as wipers. It was easier."

I laugh with him and then ask my serious question. "What did you do there in battle?"

His face loses the laughter, and his eyes take on a guarded look. "Our first task when we got there was to dig trenches. They are long and narrow ditches in the ground. It's where we had to remain, to eat and sleep."

"Goodness!" I can't hide my surprise. Imagine living in a ditch.

"It was muddy and not very hygienic," Amit continues. "The Germans had their trenches at the opposite end of the battlefield and the area in the middle was known as no man's land."

"How did you spend the days?"

"We cleaned our weapons, our gas masks and our helmets. We also slept, drank tea and played cards. We could only sleep during the afternoon in daylight and for one hour each at night."

"Oh."

"Do you know what my favourite thing was? Hot-water bottles."

I am surprised. "Hot-water bottles?"

"It was extremely cold in the trenches, especially at night."

"Ah I see. It must have been hard."

"It was, but a soldier must bear hardship. He defends those who need defending."

I nod.

"Do you know what else I did?" He does not wait for my answer. "I wrote letters. Lots and lots of letters to my mother and my sweetheart. They are both waiting for me back in my village in Punjab."

"And you will see them both very soon."

Amit nods, and I can tell that he is emotional now because his eyes are shining with tears and he keeps swallowing. There must be a lump in his throat. I change the subject.

"How did you get injured?"

"On the battlefield. A shell exploded a few feet from me. If I had stepped out first, I would have been dead. Adil, my friend and owner of the notebook, took the full blast of it. I owe him my life and…" He stops mid-sentence. He is talking about those dear to him again. I do not push to hear more and allow him to compose himself.

"I was in and out of consciousness for days. I lay where I fell on the field. I dared not move in case I was targeted with bullets from the other side. It is always better to play dead. I could see Adil. His face was turned towards me. I knew he was dead. His eyes were wide open. He didn't blink even once. I kept blinking to remind myself that I was alive. I don't know how long I lay there.

"The stretcher-bearers came. They were like angels, those two young boys. They told me afterwards that they were from a place called Bolton. I do not know where that is. They carried me to the field hospital. One fellow said this notebook was lying next to me. He assumed it was mine and picked it up. It must have fallen out of Adil's pocket when he fell to the ground with the impact of the shell."

A tear trickles down his face. I wish now that I hadn't asked him about the battlefield. It was so selfish of me to push him to relive the most traumatic experience of his life. We sit in silence for a while, and I rack my brain for something else to say. Amit, however, returns to the topic of the best friend he has lost.

"Adil and I grew up together. We come from the same village. We Muslims and Sikhs live together. On the day of our departure, our mothers stood side by side wearing matching white shalwar kameez, with dupattas on their heads. They both cried and wanted to know why we had to go so far away for war. We promised we would return."

More tears trickle down his face.

"How will I face Adil's mother when I return alone?" he sobs. "Two left from our village. Only one will return. The other will lie forever in a foreign land, away from his family and his ancestral fields. Nobody will pray for his soul's peace at his grave on the Muslim holy day of Friday, or on their Eid festivals. He will just lie in the ground with the others, forgotten."

"I don't think the soldiers will be forgotten," I say gently. "We will remember them."

Amit lowers his head, burying it into his neck as his shoulders heave. He has fully broken down now. I reach over and take his hand in my own, hoping that my touch will bring him some comfort.

Chapter 26

A Princess Again

1914–15

I enter the ward and immediately notice a change in the atmosphere. The soldiers are all gawking at me. I have been on the receiving end of that inquisitive stare all my life and recognize that it is linked to my identity.

Walking over to Amit, I smile down at him.

"Good morning," I say pleasantly.

He stares at me, his mouth opening and closing. I stifle the urge to giggle. I know what he wants to ask me, and I let him take his time.

Finally, he blurts, "There is a rumour going around that you are the Maharaja Ranjit Singh's granddaughter. Is that true?"

I smile. "Do I look like a princess?"

My response throws him. "Not in that uniform, no." He pauses. "Are you?"

"I am Princess Sophia Duleep Singh."

Amit pulls his sheet up to his chin and stares at me, wide-eyed. "Your Highness … I … forgive me … I am in a state of undress…"

I bite my lip to stop the laughter. His reaction to me is way over the top and funny. I soon find that all the soldiers behave in the same way. They are absolutely shocked that I, the granddaughter of Maharaja Ranjit Singh, am here in a Red Cross uniform, nursing them.

"My mother won't believe me," Amit keeps repeating.

To convince his mother, I have gifted him a signed photograph of me. Of course, Amit could not keep quiet about it and showed all his comrades and then they wanted one too. So here I am, signing photographs for men who will take them home to India.

In the middle of my nursing days, I receive the most unusual but most wonderful news. Bamba writes to inform me that she has married an English gentleman doctor in India. He is called Richard Sutherland.

I must say that I am extremely surprised. I thought she would have chosen a Sikh man. She was always trying to get me to marry one. I still remember those terrible drawings she sent me. Anyway, I am so pleased she is happy.

"Princess, how lovely to see you again."

Professor Kumar, my friend from the sea voyage back from India, greets me with a broad smile. He has come on a day trip to Brighton to spend the afternoon with me. We have remained in touch over the years, and I am so pleased to see him. He has the answers to my questions, many of which are about history, and he also keeps me up to date on what is happening in India. There seems to be an increase in rebellious feelings among Indians, who are demanding that the British leave India.

I suspect Bamba is a part of this Indian nationalist movement, but she doesn't reveal anything in her letters to me. She knows that they may well be intercepted by the India Office, forever suspicious of us Duleep Singhs, children of a rebel maharaja. I suppose the India Office does have a point. Bamba is a rebel. She is Papa's true heir and the only one of us who inherited our grandmother Maharani Jindan's spirit.

"So where have you been since the war started?" I ask the professor.

"I've been down on the south coast trying to help with

the hospitals there," he replies. "So many injured soldiers. It is quite upsetting to witness their trauma. I fear the effects of the shells dropped around them has made them ghosts."

I nod gravely.

"You know, there was an interesting character that I came across at the hospital," the professor says. "I met his wife first as she was on the wards every day, and then the man himself."

"Who?"

"He is an Indian lawyer. We got chatting, as he studied law in England before moving to South Africa to set up a law firm."

Young Indian students and lawyers were nothing new in London. The city was full of them. Neither was the fact that this man lived in South Africa. Travel to different parts of the Empire was common for those who could afford it.

"What was so special about him?" I ask. "You seem a little fixated on him."

Mr Kumar shrugs. "I don't know. He was a small man, thin, and on first glance quite unremarkable. Then he began to speak, and I realized that in fact, he was quite remarkable. He certainly knows how to hold one's attention. I suppose it's his barrister skills."

"What did he say?"

"He said that the support for the war from the Indians would mean that Britain would be grateful for their sacrifice and release India from the Empire. He is quite convinced of it. That is why he is here in England, nursing the soldiers back to health."

I bite my lip. The man sounds very much like Emmeline, who also believes that support for the war will mean a reward at the end.

"Emmeline has a deal with Mr Asquith that he will grant the vote to women if we support the war," I say. "Does this man have a deal with the Viceroy of India or Asquith himself?"

Doubt covers the professor's face. "I don't think so."

I make an attempt not to roll my eyes. I saw as a little girl how my papa had tried to take back his kingdom. The people who had used him and convinced him that the mighty British Empire would leave Punjab so that he may retake his rightful place as ruler. I think this little skinny man the professor is talking about must be quite deluded. He will die a disappointed man, just like my papa.

"What was his name?" I ask.

"Gandhi."

Chapter 27

Victory

1916–20

6 February 1918

It seems we have won a battle, but not the war.

Yet.

I'm not referring to the war with Imperial Germany.

I'm talking about the war for women's votes.

A few of us suffragettes are standing outside the gates of Parliament waiting for news. A new prime minister, David Lloyd George, has replaced that horrid Asquith, and he has decided that it is time for women to receive the vote. But it will not be all women. It will only be those over the age of thirty who own property, and the wives of men who own property.

The Members of Parliament are voting right now.

"Lloyd George has noticed the women's contribution to the war and believes it is right that we are given suffrage," someone in the crowd says.

I feel like answering that women have been holding the fort for centuries whilst men have gone off to war to kill each other, but I hold my tongue. This is a day to celebrate our first major victory.

Ada comes running from her position outside one of the entrances. "It's passed! It's passed! We've got the vote!"

We hug and laugh.

At last!

The Representation of the People Act of 1918 passes.

Two years ago on the 4 August 1916 I had the most amount of fun on Our Day. This was the 46th anniversary of the British Red Cross when people were asked to donate money. Nearly everybody I know wore Red Cross pins on their lapels and collars.

I led the efforts for the Indian troops by setting up a stall with my friends in Haymarket. My stall was the brightest and prettiest, with colourful silk sheet decorations. All my volunteer friends, both English and Indian, wore traditional Indian clothes.

The success of that day gave me the idea for 'India Day', where I intend to raise money solely for the Indian troops.

In typical fashion, the India Office is trying to thwart my plans. Sometimes I think they only exist to make my life a misery. I can just imagine the over-promoted schemers rubbing their hands and saying, "Oh, look! Princess Sophia is doing something useful and kind for mankind – how can we spoil her good efforts?"

Honestly, what is wrong with raising funds for men who need basic items like solid shoes to protect against water and mud, and clothes that will keep out the cold? These men are willing to risk life and limb for King and Country, so why object to providing for them?

It breaks my heart when I think of the terrible conditions at the front. I am quite determined to build huts for the men so that they may have shelter against the cold, wind and snow. And I think chocolate and cigarettes would be welcomed by them, too.

I have all these plans and the horrid India Office is trying to thwart me. I share my frustrations with my friend Ada when we meet up for a cup of tea and chat.

"But what's stopping you from going ahead with India Day?" she asks.

"I can't do it without a licence," I moan. "I applied to the Metropolitan Police but due to my status as a princess, they passed it on to the India Office."

She narrows her eyes over the rim of the teacup. "Is that so bad?"

"It is the one place that has viewed me with deep suspicion since my papa's rebellion against the Crown," I admit. "It is clear to me that they don't want an Indian princess to be the saviour of the Indian troops."

"Well, don't give up," she says. "You're doing a valuable thing. Men in suits are always trying to stop women from doing what they want to do. It's almost like they have nothing better to engage their time."

I take a large bite of my cake. She's right. I shall soldier on.

It is a good thing I dug my heels in, because the following day I receive good news. India Day can go ahead and furthermore, I am offered the position of honorary secretary for the event. The event will be held under the banner of the YMCA: this stands for 'Young Men's Christian Association'. This fine organization already does so much for all our troops.

I do not stress myself over the change of heart from the authorities. I am just glad to have the licence, although

I am a little annoyed that I haven't been granted permission to include elephants in my street procession. I do think the grand, majestic animals would have helped me raise more money.

Goodness me!

The India Office may hate me but I am valued elsewhere, it seems.

To my utter shock, I receive a public letter from Field Marshal Lord John French, the commander-in-chief of the British Expeditionary Force. He thanks me for my efforts for the Indian troops and goes on to say that the soldiers under his command at Ypres splendidly upheld the glorious fighting tradition of the Indian army… "It will always be a source of pride and happiness that I have been associated in the field with these gallant troops."

It gets better. A few days later, *The Times* newspaper covers the story by printing:

"Princess Sophia Duleep Singh, who is organizing the India Day celebrations in London next Friday September 20, has received a letter from Lord French in which he pays tribute to…"

We end up raising so much money that I can now pay for 50,000 huts for the Indian troops at the front. I wish them all warmth and comfort as they defend us against the enemy.

11 November 1918

We have won the war.

Imperial Germany is devastated and defeated. People say the country will never be able to rise again.

The Indian soldiers start to depart for their homeland. They thank me for my nursing care, and I try not to cry. One by one, they all leave to rejoin their families.

Now that the war is over, I suddenly feel lonely without my sisters. I'm going to try and persuade Catherine to return to England. She's been living in Switzerland, a neutral country, for the duration of the war and it's time she came home.

14 December 1918

I'm dressed in my suffragette colours. Ada, Gertrude and I walk hand-in-hand up the stairs to the school.

This is it.

The day has finally arrived.

This is the one that we, the suffragettes, have fought for with all our hearts.

The prime minister, David Lloyd George, has called a general election. As a woman over the age of thirty with property to my name, I am legally permitted to cast my vote.

"Ladies." The clerk smiles at us from behind the table. He is a cheerful-looking man. "Names, please?"

"Princess Sophia Duleep Singh," I reply with a smile.

The clerk almost stands to attention before fumbling with sheets of paper. "This is your ballot paper. Please place an 'X' against the candidate of your choice."

"Thank you." I take the paper and glance around. "Should I go into any booth?"

He nods. "You will find a pencil inside."

I glide forward, feeling light on my feet. Taking a deep breath and knowing that this moment will forever be etched in my memory, I mark an 'X' against my chosen candidate. As I emerge from the booth, I think of all the ladies in the land who will vote for Mr Lloyd George's party. He supported us. We shall support him.

Ada, Gertrude and I exchange a smile when we emerge from our individual booths.

It feels surreal.

We have finally done it.

But it is not over.

Now we must fight for all the other women left behind.

1920

The Indian sun scorches my face, but I remain steadfast in my position.

With the war over, I found it hard to fill my time. There was not much to occupy my days, and I think it showed in my letters to India. That is why Bamba insisted that I pay her a visit.

I did so willingly, keen to get away from dreary London for now.

And here I am now, standing in the relentless heat by a river in western India. Bamba and I have travelled here with a single purpose.

This is where our grandmother Maharani Jindan was cremated in 1864 – far, far away from her native Punjab. At the time, Papa arranged for a small tomb to contain his mother's ashes. We are standing before the tomb now, as a Sikh man recites a prayer.

Bamba and I are taking our grandmother's ashes home. Rather than leave her here all alone, Maharani Jindan's earthly remains will be stored in the same mausoleum in Lahore that holds our grandfather's ashes.

We are doing right by our grandmother.

It is time to end her exile.

Chapter 28

For All Women

1928

Today is 2 July 1928.

I stand in Parliament Square with my close friends Ada and Gertrude. Una Dugdale, who introduced me to the suffragette movement all those years ago at a weekend party, is also with us. We hold hands and breathe the air, savouring the final victory. This, I imagine, is how soldiers feel on the battlefield after the other side has waved the white flag and accepted defeat.

It has taken us years to get to this point but we have made it. The 1918 Representation Act which allowed women over thirty with property to vote was never going to be enough for us. And so we carried on with the fight.

A few months after the Rep Act in 1918, the Parliament Qualification for Women Act was passed which permitted women to stand as Members of Parliament. The first woman to win a seat in the 1918 election was Constance Markievicz. She, however, refused to take her place in Parliament as she represented Sinn Fein, the Irish nationalist party that wants independence from Britain. The first woman to actually take her seat inside Parliament was Nancy Astor. She won her husband's parliamentary seat in Plymouth when he had to stand down at the death of his Viscount father. As the new Viscount, Nancy's husband inherited a seat in the House of Lords.

My friends and I weren't really sure about Nancy at first. I mean she had never been part of our suffragette movement, so we didn't know if she would fight for the rest of us. But she did, and she became a big supporter of the women's movement from within the parliamentary walls.

There were other advancements too. In 1919, a new law, the Sex Disqualification (Removal) Act, prohibited women from being excluded from employment. That meant women could join any profession. I can't help wishing that this law had been around when Bamba had lived here. Perhaps she would have qualified as a doctor in England and not left me for India.

The campaigning continued, not the violent type from before the Great War, but political meetings and pressure on the government. Finally in 1927, the prime minister, Stanley Baldwin, pledged to give the vote to all women. There was opposition, of course. Some men (and women) thought women under thirty without property (as in young and poor) could not be trusted to play a part in deciding the country's leaders.

Our old adversary, Mr Winston Churchill, who was Home Secretary on that awful day, Black Friday, is still a government minister. He was completely against expanding the right to vote. Thankfully, he was in the minority in the Houses of Parliament and there were more members who supported us.

Anyway, enough about Mr Churchill and the men like him who tried to deny us women our rights. They have lost the fight and I want to focus on today.

My gaze rests upon Westminster Hall, which is the oldest part of the Houses of Parliament. They say it was built a few years after William the Conqueror won the Battle of Hastings in 1066. It was his son, William Rufus, who built the hall and it still stands today, nearly a thousand years later.

So many historic events have occurred in Westminster Hall. It held the trial of Charles I, the king who had his head chopped off, and also the trial of Guy Fawkes, a member of the Gunpowder Plot to blow up Parliament. The hall has even held celebrations, notably the coronation feast of the doomed Tudor queen, Anne Boleyn.

There should have been a celebration there today, for it is a historic date.

Today we won the women's war.

The law that permits all women over the age of twenty-one to vote has finally been passed.

It is called the Representation of the People (Equal Franchise) Act.

1928 will forever be remembered as the year that British women were finally recognized as equal citizens of their country.

We shall be able to have our say in the laws that govern us.

We have achieved our freedom.

I just wish our friend and leader Emmeline had lived to see this day. It is one of life's tragedies that she died only weeks before her final dream could be realized. On the 14 June 1928, Emmeline took her last breath. She was sixty-nine years old. I was devastated at the loss of such a good friend. We all were. Ada, Gertrude, Una and I were amongst thousands that walked behind her coffin, dressed in our suffragette white with purple sashes. It was at Brompton Cemetery, her final resting place, that we decided that we would take a walk outside Parliament on the day of our final victory.

And here we now are.

"I think one day," Ada says, "the Houses of Parliament will have a painting or statue of Emmeline within its walls."

Gertrude nods. "She has made her place in history and she will never be forgotten."

"What about us?" Una asks.

I squeeze her hand. "I think you will be remembered in history as the first woman to refuse to say 'I obey' in your wedding vows in church."

Una grins. "It will do."

We are silent again, each of us lost in our own thoughts.

My mind returns to Una's question. Will we be remembered? Will future generations of women and girls care that we fought for their human right to vote and be counted? Perhaps they will, perhaps they won't. I don't think I mind either way. The important thing for me is that I have achieved my life's purpose for the advancement of women.

I have done my part.

The ones who will come after me will continue the fight for women's advancement in their own way.

Author's note

I have been sharing the story of Princess Sophia Duleep Singh with children from the moment I heard the writer and broadcaster Anita Anand speak about the suffragette. Sophia takes prime position with the World War II heroine spy, Noor-Un-Nissa Inayat Khan, in my Girls' Rights workshops in schools. Both British, both of South Asian heritage, both princesses, and both role models that ALL British children should know about for their historical contribution to Britain.

Growing up, I hardly ever read about women who looked like me in the history books. This was not because women of colour were not present at historical events. It is simply because their roles, their contributions and their stories were not written down by our historians. I hope we can change this and be more inclusive of our shared history.

Sophia's life, of course, was not just about her suffragette activities. She was also a Red Cross nurse, taking care of the Indian soldiers in Brighton hospitals. A total of 1.3 million Indian soldiers travelled from India to Europe to fight for their King-Emperor in the Great War. Adil represents the 62,000 who were killed in the war. Amit represents the 67,000 who were injured in battle.

As a young girl, Sophia would have thought that her father's opposition to the Empire was foolish. Yet, in Sophia's lifetime, Britain ended its rule of India in 1947. The land was divided into two new states, the Republic of India and the Islamic Republic of Pakistan. The Punjab state, which had once been the great kingdom of her grandfather, was divided between these two new nations. The division of land unleashed horrific violence and it is said that up to one million people were killed.

Sophia died peacefully in her sleep on 22 August 1948 at her home. She was seventy-two years old. Her brothers Victor and Freddie had already died, as had her sister Catherine. Princess Bamba, the last surviving child of Maharaja Duleep Singh, travelled to England from her home in the newly created country of Pakistan to oversee Sophia's funeral. Bamba had always taken care of Sophia, and she saw to it that her baby sister's last wishes were fulfilled. Although Sophia had been baptised and raised as a Christian, her final wish was to be cremated according to Sikh rites in England, and that her ashes be scattered in her ancestral land.

I would like to thank all the women who have contributed to my telling of Sophia's story for young readers. Nazima Abdillahi for backing the story from the very start. The team at Scholastic: Leah James, Elizabeth Scoggins Singh, Emily Hibbs, Rona Skene, Martha Gavin and my publicist Kiran Khanom. And of course, my agent Sophie Gorell Barnes for supporting all my stories.

A final word to my readers. At the end of the book, Sophia says, "The ones who will come after me will continue the fight for women's advancement in their own way."

Perhaps that could be you in the future?

Experience history first-hand with *My Story* –
a series of vividly imagined accounts of life in the past.

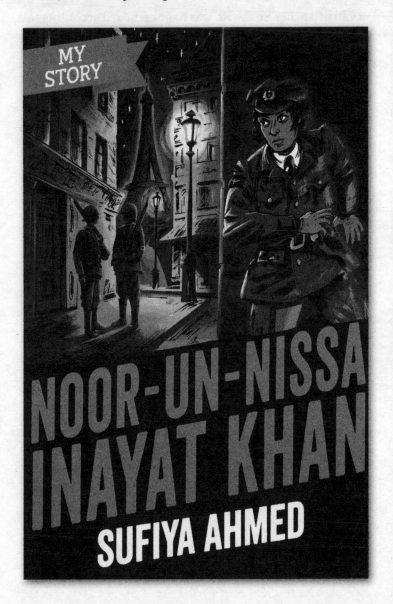

MY STORY

NOOR-UN-NISSA
INAYAT KHAN

SUFIYA AHMED

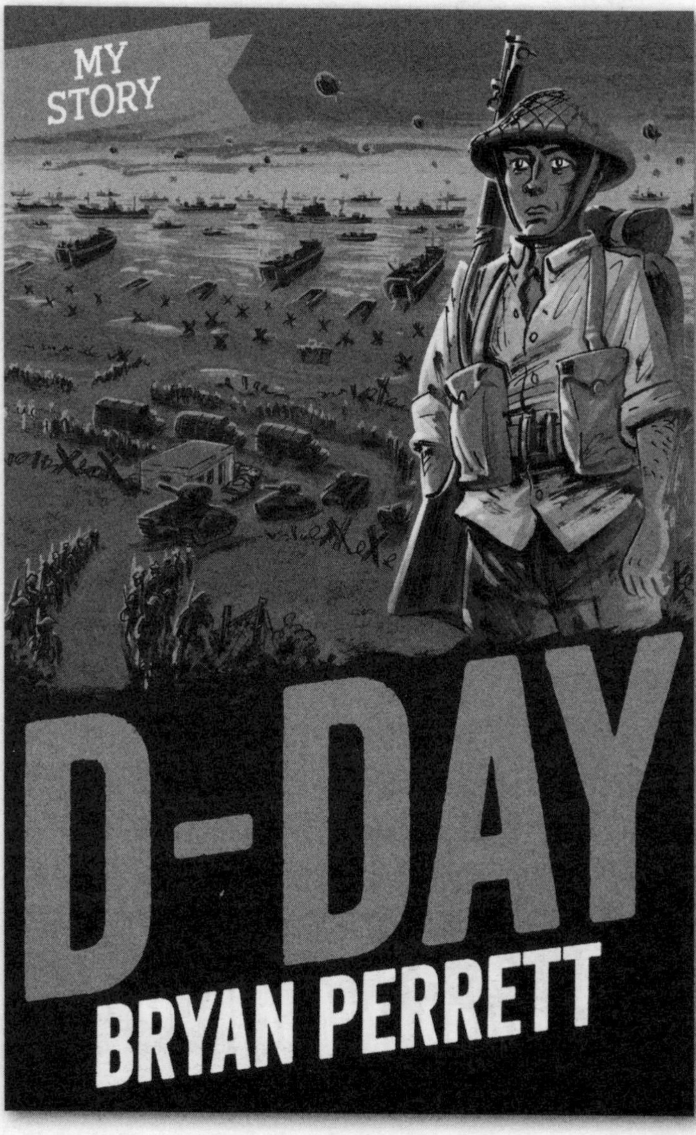
MY STORY
D-DAY
BRYAN PERRETT

MY
STORY

A PICTURE
OF FREEDOM

PATRICIA C MCKISSACK

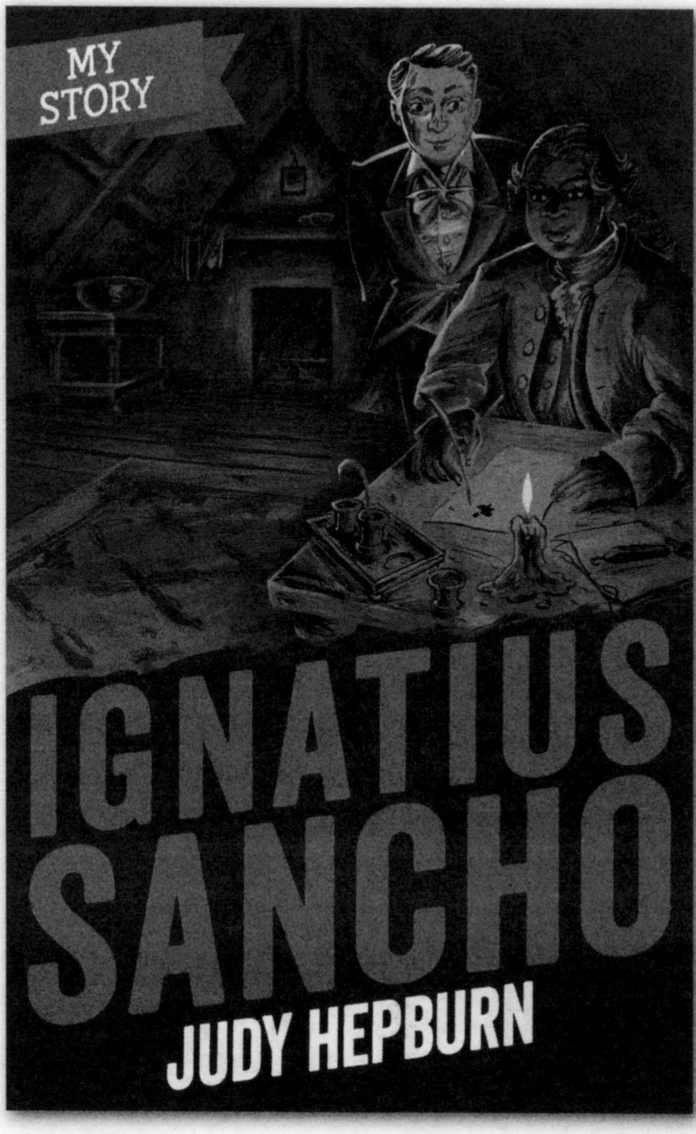
MY STORY
IGNATIUS SANCHO
JUDY HEPBURN

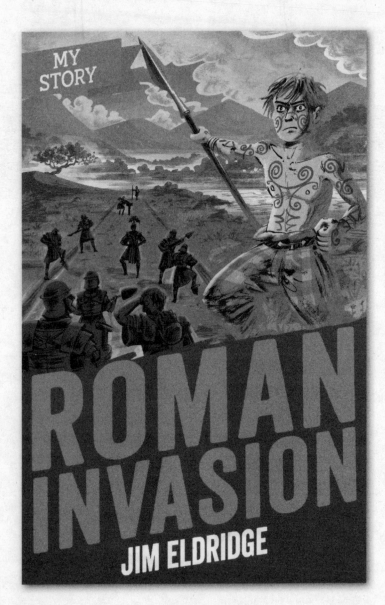